A MURDER IN BLUE

PENELOPE BANKS MURDER MYSTERIES
BOOK 13

COLETTE CLARK

Copyright © 2024 by Colette Clark

All rights reserved.

No part of this book may be reproduced in any form or by any electronic or mechanical means, including information storage and retrieval systems, without written permission from the author, except for the use of brief quotations in a book review.

ABOUT THE AUTHOR

Colette Clark lives in New York and has always enjoyed learning more about the history of her amazing city. She decided to combine that curiosity and love of learning with her addiction to reading and watching mysteries. Her first series, **Penelope Banks Murder Mysteries** is the result of those passions. When she's not writing she can be found doing Sudoku puzzles, drawing, eating tacos, visiting museums dedicated to unusual/weird/wacky things, and, of course, reading mysteries by other great authors.

Join my Newsletter to receive news about New Releases and Sales!
https://dashboard.mailerlite.com/forms/148684/72678356487767318/share

DESCRIPTION

First Class train travel never looked so deadly....

France 1926

Penelope "Pen" Banks and friends are finally headed to Paris aboard the famous Blue Train. No sooner has the train left the station than one of their group is accused of theft by another First Class passenger. The situation is quickly resolved thanks to the timely (yet rather suspicious) intervention of a fellow female passenger.

When the victim of the supposed theft is found dead later that evening, a surprising number of suspects are uncovered. There may have been more to the victim's travel plans than a simple tryst along the French Riviera with his young female companion.

Unfortunately, the accusation of theft has Penelope's friend Lulu accused as one of the suspects. Can Pen find the real culprit before the cuffs are placed when they reach the next station?

A Murder in Blue is the thirteenth book in the Penelope Banks Murder Mysteries series set in the 1920s. Join her and her friends as they continue their European adventure.

FIRST CARRIAGE

101 Penelope	102 Richard	103 Lulu	104 Benny	105 Cousin Cordelia

Jules ↓

To Front of Train — To Carriage 2

SECOND CARRIAGE

201 Thomas	202 Marie	203 Honorine	204 Aristide Barbier	205 Pierre Padou

Quentin ↓

To Carriage 1 — To Carriage 3

THIRD CARRIAGE

301 ?	302 ?	303 ?	304 Cosette	305 Lucien

Adrien ↓

To Carriage 2 — To Bar/Dining

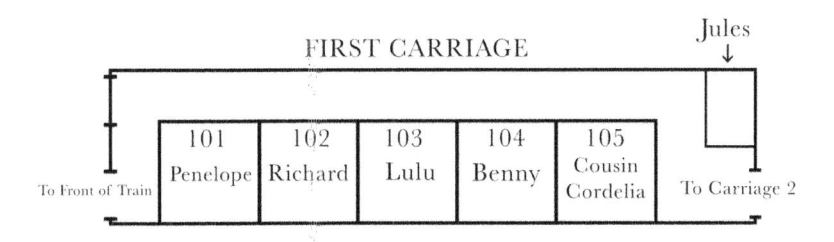

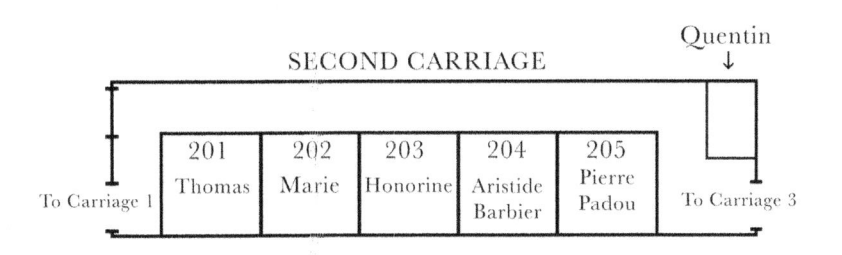

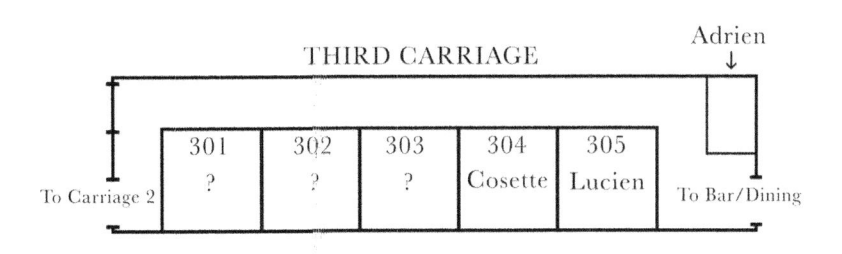

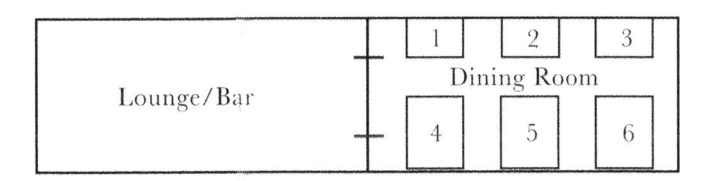

Lounge/Bar

Dining Room

1	2	3
4	5	6

1. Thomas & Marie
2. Pierre Padou
3. Aristide Barbier & Cosette
4. Penelope, Richard, André, Simon
5. Honorine, Lulu, Benny, Cousin Cordelia
6. Lucien

CHAPTER ONE

NICE 1926

"Benny, I'll kill you if we miss this train!" Penelope "Pen" Banks could have positively strangled her friend Benjamin Davenport, what with his insistence on dropping into one more quaint little bar or shop before their departure from Nice.

After a tragic start to their summer in Antibes, the rest of their stay along the Côte d'Azur had passed rather pleasantly for Penelope and her friends. They'd spent the past week in Nice, in preparation for their departure to Paris—earlier than expected. Thank goodness they'd had all their luggage sent ahead with the others in their party: her Cousin Cordelia, Lucille "Lulu" Simmons, and Penelope's fiancé Richard Prescott.

Of course, that would do them no good should they miss their train!

"Oh, garter your stockings, dove," Benny said with the same nonchalance that he treated everything in life. "We have First Class tickets, they'll hold it for us."

"I'll garter you if they don't!" They both knew that First Class tickets or not, the train waited for no one.

Benny laughed as his longer legs kept pace with hers in Cuban heels while they sped through the station. Blessedly, there wasn't much traffic that late in the evening, so there were few obstacles to delay them: a couple on a bench practically entangled with one another, obviously in no hurry to catch a train; an employee of the station leisurely reading the paper and smoking a cigarette; and a family of five in which the mother was arguing with the father while the older boy, about nine, and two younger girls looked on with worried expressions. Each one was like a photograph permanently pasted into the album of Penelope's mind, as she had the strange ability to recall everything she saw in perfect detail.

Penelope slowed down as their train came into view. She marveled at how truly stunning it was even at night. The lights of the station bounced off the rich blue steel exterior with gold trim and lettering announcing the company that owned the line.

"Come, come, dove, no stopping now!" Benny teased, quickly walking past her.

Penelope caught up to him and showed their tickets to the uniformed representative standing near the first car. She had booked five single sleeping compartments for their entire group, even though it was only an overnight trip. They announced themselves and showed their tickets.

"Our friends and luggage should already be on board."

"*Bien*," he said with a slight bow. "You are in carriage two. Follow me, s'il vous plaît."

Penelope exhaled to calm her breath and present the proper sort of image for a woman traveling aboard the finest train France had to offer. She had specifically dressed for the occasion, in a smart yellow frock with large polkadots and a matching hat.

They were handed off to a concierge dedicated to the first of the three First Class carriages. He was a trim man in his thirties, with a tidy little mustache the same dark shade as his hair underneath a cap. He wore a dark blue uniform with gold embellishments along the cuff and lapels, which almost matched the colors of the train. It was buttoned over a crisp white dress shirt with a starched collar. He helped them up into the car, then took their tickets.

"Bonsoir, Monsieur Davenport, Mademoiselle Banks, my name is Jules and I shall be your personal concierge during your voyage. I am located here at the head of the car, and can accommodate almost any of your travel needs." He gestured to the small compartment at the end of the carriage that housed a padded seat and an upper and lower cabinet containing most of those needs, including a silver champagne bucket waiting to be filled, should the desire arise. They really were quite prepared. "Your luggage has already been placed in your corresponding compartments."

It was understandable that such an impressive company would not only have a conductor, quaintly called a concierge on this line, for each of the three First Class cars. Naturally, he'd memorized the names of which passenger was in each compartment for his own car well ahead of time.

Not one minute after they had entered the corridor, at exactly 8:00 p.m. a final whistle announced their departure, and Penelope breathed a sigh of relief. They *had* cut it quite close. Through the windows along the corridor, she watched the station move in the opposite direction.

The interior of the car was richly decorated, with mahogany wood and brass fixtures. The lush carpet that quieted their steps was in the same rich blue as the exterior of the train, with a pattern of gold crests. Jules led them past

3

the solidly built doors of each compartment numbered 101 to 105.

"Mademoiselle Banks, you have compartment 101," Jules opened the door for her, then handed her the key with a dark blue fob and gold numbering.

Penelope had chosen this cabin specifically because it had a door that led to Richard's in 102. She assumed the two compartments further down also shared dual doors, should passengers be so inclined. Of course, both parties had to agree to the conspiracy, each opening their respective door to the other. Pen and Richard were very much inclined. Lulu and Benny were in 103 and 104 respectively and would no doubt get up to their own kind of shenanigans at night, a round of gossip or a game of cards. Cousin Cordelia had the last room right next to the concierge station, which would set her easily frayed nerves at ease.

Pen saw that her personal overnight luggage had indeed been placed in her sleeper room. The rest was assuredly in the storage carriage. The only thing she really needed for this short trip were her toiletries, a nightgown, a robe, a change of clothes for the morning, and a book to read before bed. She wondered if even that latter item would be necessary, smiling to herself as she thought of Richard.

"If you wish, I can turn down your bed now. However, I am happy to wait until after you've enjoyed your dinner service."

"The couch is perfectly fine for now," Penelope said.

"For now," Benny purred.

"Very good, mademoiselle," Jules said, politely ignoring Benny's suggestive taunting. He gestured to a button on the wall in between the couch and the door. "If you need anything at all, simply push this button and I shall come instantly, unless I am otherwise engaged to help another guest. In that case, all concierges are alerted and one of them may come in my place."

"Wonderful," Penelope said with a bright smile indicating she was happily set for now.

"As mentioned, there will be a dinner service, which is at nine. The dining room is located in the fourth carriage. However, the bar and lounge area in the same car is always open and staffed."

"Smashing!" Benny said. Penelope couldn't fault the sentiment. She felt like having a drink herself after that mad dash.

When Jules and Benny left to see him to his compartment, Pen took a moment to admire her accommodations. The room was done in various shades of blue with gold touches. The carpet was the same as the corridor, but the upholstery was a more subtle shade, with tiny dark blue and gold flowers. The curtains were a light blue with gold fringe. On the small table underneath the window sat a little lamp. She left it off so she could have a better view after she opened the curtains. It was too dark to see anything of the Mediterranean as they sped along the coast to their next stop in Cannes , but she left them open all the same. There was a knock at the door leading to room 102, and Penelope smiled.

"Who is it?" Pen sang.

"Just a stranger in the night, wondering if you'd like company."

"Oh, I don't think my fiancé would like that very much. You see, he's joining me on this voyage. In fact, I believe he's reserved the very room you seem to be occupying."

"In that case, you'd better let me in before he comes back."

Penelope laughed and opened the door. The man

staring back at her with a grin was half a head taller than her, even in her small heels. He had dark eyes with lush lashes and strong features that made him devilishly handsome. Even the burn scar rising from the right side of his collar up his neck and ending just below his right ear couldn't take away from that. Considering he'd earned it fighting in the Great War, it made him seem that much more dashing.

"Why, you look an awful lot like my fiancé, Richard Prescott. I should warn you, he's a detective with the New York Police Department in case you're thinking of doing something inappropriate."

"Well, thank goodness we're here in France," Richard said, grinning as he shamelessly brought her closer to him and kissed her.

Penelope smiled against his lips. It remained even after they separated. "It's a shame we only have one night on this train. This situation is awfully convenient."

"Then we'll have to make the most of the night." Richard arched a brow. "I was beginning to think you wouldn't make it."

"Blame Benny for that. Of course, it's my fault for indulging his whims. There were just too many open stalls hawking their wares and he does love to shop."

"Perhaps you all should have stayed here while I met my friends in Paris?"

"Would you have preferred that?" Pen asked with uncertainty. Richard had received a message about some of his old war friends having a reunion of sorts in Paris and decided to leave earlier than their expected departure date. Penelope had suggested going with him, which had everyone else deciding to join as well. Fortunately, she had changed their original tickets early enough to have the entire car for their party.

"Perish the thought, my dear."

He sounded sincere, which was reassuring. Penelope certainly had no plans on interfering with his reunion, which was sure to be an uncensored reminiscing of war exploits. The presence of a woman would certainly damper the atmosphere. Pen had no quarrel with shopping and visiting museums to compensate.

"You made it on board and that's all that matters. How about a cocktail before dinner? Your cousin and Lucille are already there. I told them, I'd wait for you."

"How considerate you are. I'm sure Benny has already beat us to them."

"Then we should go before they drink the bar out of alcohol."

They left the door between the compartments open and exited through Penelope's door. They had to pass through the second and third carriages to get to the lounge car. In the passageway between carriages, there was a little window that looked into the next car, giving them a view of the corridor. They were so narrow, Pen assumed it was to alert people passing through that there was already someone coming or going. Right then, that view into the next car was blocked by a rather debonair man sticking a cigarette in his mouth. He lit it with an onyx lighter that had a silver emblem of a rearing horse that looked quite valuable. He turned to look at them while he took his first drag. His eyes lingered on Penelope, and he grinned around his cigarette.

"Bonsoir, cherie," he said after exhaling a cloud of smoke.

Pen flashed a smile and hurried on, eager to get away from the smell and that leering look. The man patently ignored Richard, who gave him a hard look before following Pen.

As they continued through the second and third cars, they noticed there were no concierges in either carriage. When they neared the fourth carriage, they could understand why.

"It's gone! *Volé!*" A man's voice boomed so loudly that Penelope and Richard could hear him, even through the closed doors of each car. Translating that final word, Pen understood that something of his had been stolen.

The two hurried their step to see what was happening in the lounge. They were presented with a man, perhaps in his early fifties, nearly red in the face as he continued to rage. He was short in stature and his hairline had receded too much to avoid covering the shiny dome that gleamed in the low light of the car. He was quite nicely dressed in a well-tailored suit and fine shoes.

A much younger, and much more attractive woman stood next to him, an exasperated look on her face. Her short blonde hair was done in perfect finger waves and pinned back on one side with a trio of bobby pins. Penelope recognized the Edward Molyneux dress she had on, from the Spring Collection. She was temporarily dazzled by the stunning beaded design. The hemline was high enough to match modern trends, done in a sheer cream color with a low-cut overdress. Mademoiselle was certainly very well-kept.

One concierge was already there, trying to play the diplomat. He was younger than Jules, with light brown hair and a cleanly shaven face. A third, much older concierge emerged from the lavatory in the lounge area, looking quite alarmed at the commotion taking place during his brief absence. Jules stepped in to provide support as the youngest of the three tried to calm the man, speaking in French. "*Monsieur Barbier, please calm down.*"

"*I will not!*" Monsieur Barbier spat back at him, also in French. "*My wallet has been stolen and someone on this train has it!*"

There were only a handful of people in the lounge. Pen briefly noted Lulu and Benny at the bar, paused in ordering their drinks to observe the scene the man was causing. Cousin Cordelia was seated at a small table further on, a snifter of cognac already in front of her. She had her hand clutched at her collar as she stared wide-eyed at the ranting man.

Other than Penelope's friends, there were two men in suits. They looked on with mild interest, the older one idly smoking a cigar.

"*I demand a search of everyone present.*" Monsieur Barbier's beady eyes fell on Lulu with suspicion. "*Starting with this one. It was no doubt she who took it. She is exactly the sort.*"

Although Penelope's friend wasn't fluent in French, Lulu didn't need a translator to recognize the look in Monsieur Barbier's eyes. She was no doubt used to being unfairly targeted due to her race. Fortunately, she had several friends to champion her honor, and they all spoke up at once.

"Now see here," Benny said, speaking English for Lulu's sake. He took a step to insert himself between the man and Lulu.

"I doubt my friend stole anything from you," Penelope added, strutting across the lounge toward her friend.

She was quickly followed by Richard, who voiced his own objection, also in French, "*Do you have any proof of this supposed theft?*"

The man responded in accented English, realizing he was surrounded by Americans. "The proof is that my wallet was stolen. If this woman didn't take it, then who did?"

"Miss Simmons has been sitting here with me this entire time," Cousin Cordelia insisted, her voice filled with umbrage.

Before anyone could protest further, they were interrupted by the sound of a woman's voice, in English but with a definite French accent. It came from the entrance leading to the First Class sleeper cars. "What is this now?"

They all turned to see an attractive woman, in her early to mid forties. She looked around the room with beautiful dark, glittering eyes that held a hint of mischief. In her hand was a leather wallet. "It seems I've arrived to a bit of a fracas? I was hoping to return this wallet I found lying in the corridor to its rightful owner."

CHAPTER TWO

"*That wallet belongs to me!*" Monsieur Barbier shouted in French, rushing over to the latest arrival in the lounge car. "*How did you get your hands on it?*"

"*Ah,*" the woman said, flicking the wallet in her hand out of reach at the last minute. She arched a brow as she added, "*But how can I be assured it is yours, Monsieur?*"

"*Why you little—*"

"*Madame DuBois, please,*" said the younger concierge in a weary voice as he walked over to intercede.

Madame DuBois pursed her lips in a surprisingly coquettish manner for someone her age. It had the effect of charming even Penelope, who couldn't hold back her smile at how insouciant the woman was. She reminded Pen a bit of herself.

"Don't you suppose he owes Mademoiselle an apology?" Madame DuBois said in English, giving both men a pout as her eyes flicked to Lulu.

"I most certainly will not!" Monsieur Barbier said. He quickly shot Lulu a hard glare, as though she was conspiring with this woman to keep him from his wallet. He turned back to her. "You passed us in the corridor, brushed right by me. That's when you picked my pocket! Admit it!"

"Or perhaps that's simply when it fell out? Thankfully, I was there to recover it," she replied with a pert smile.

"May I please have the wallet, Madame DuBois?" The concierge asked, also in English now for everyone's benefit.

Madame DuBois simply arched a brow and waited, practically daring either of them to make a grab for the wallet. She insolently tapped it against the back of her right shoulder as she waited.

"*Is that all you intend to do about this, Quentin?*" Monsieur Barbier sputtered in anger at the young concierge. "*What am I paying a First Class ticket for?*"

"Now, now, it is hardly the concierge's fault that your wallet has been...*misplaced*." All eyes turned to a new party to the confrontation. It was the same man Penelope had seen smoking in the passageway. Everyone had been so consumed by the spectacle, they hadn't even noticed him enter. He swanned over, giving Madame DuBois a knowing smile. He shifted his eyes to linger again on Penelope, then settle even longer on Monsieur Barbier's companion, who had nothing to offer but disinterest in return. He continued in English, with a conspicuous French accent he used to a rather suave effect, as he addressed the *monsieur* himself. "I believe your anger is misplaced, Monsieur. It seems you have accused not one but two beautiful women of a crime."

"Who are you to interfere?" Monsieur Barbier demanded.

"Monsieur Lucien Vollant," he replied. He took hold of the hand of the beautiful young companion and kissed the back of it before she quickly snatched it away in offense.

"Perhaps it *might* be considerate for you to apologize?" Penelope said, drawing Monsieur Barbier's attention before another tempest ensued. "It seems your accusation of my friend was unfounded, monsieur."

"I agree," Madame DuBois said, grinning at Penelope. "You have also been rather rude in your demands for the wallet. I would think a please and thank you is in order?"

Monsieur Barbier looked around in outrage, hoping someone might offer a counter-opinion in his favor. The young woman accompanying him stared with a helpless expression. The two gentlemen still seated at the far end of the lounge were back to minding their own business, patently ignoring the scene. Quentin, the young concierge, seemed unsure of who might take most offense if he intervened. Jules was set to say something but Monsieur Barbier spoke before he could.

"I'll do no such thing," he hissed, turning his anger back on Madame DuBois. He reached around and angrily snatched the wallet from her. She simply sighed and shrugged, even as he quickly opened it to scan the contents, making sure everything was still there.

"*Come, Cosette,*" he said, switching back to French and grabbing the wrist of the pretty young woman with him.

"*Cosette?*" Lucien mused, giving her a leering look. "*Such a pretty name for such a pretty woman.*"

Penelope supposed it was a pretty enough name for a very pretty young woman, but it also seemed awfully precious. Her parents almost invited such inappropriate comments by giving her such a coquettish name. Monsieur Barbier gave Madame DuBois one final glare before stomping back to a table without so much as a thank you, dragging her with him.

"*Thank you, Madame DuBois,*" Quentin said begrudgingly, giving a final nod before returning to his designated car. Jules and the other concierge followed, both giving one last wary glance to the passengers in the lounge to make sure everything truly was settled.

"You're very welcome," Madame DuBois sang in a teasing voice to Monsieur Barbier as she sauntered toward the bar. "You should take better care of your wallet, sir. It's no wonder you have yet to buy your young lady friend a ring, being so negligent with your money."

Monsieur Barbier's nostrils flared in outrage. Penelope wondered if part of it was her use of English, so even the woman he had first accused could understand it. His young lady friend shot Madame DuBois a look of haughty contempt, which only made her laugh. Penelope *had* noted the lack of a wedding ring on either of them, though the monsieur had a hint of an indentation where a ring had left its mark prior to removal. It was quite obvious that Monsieur Barbier's traveling companion was not his wife.

"Even in French I would have understood that suggestion," Lulu said with one side of her mouth hitched in a smirk.

"Ah, Americans, some of my favorite people," said Madame DuBois, clapping her hands together. She had a light French lilt, pegging her as a native Frenchwoman, but her English was perfect.

Pen studied her as she swiveled to quickly order a glass of champagne from the bar. Her dark hair was in a French side-part bob, the waved hair swinging every way she turned her head. Her mouth was set in a playful manner, perpetually hinting at some bit of private amusement. She was stylishly svelte, wearing a chic, loose-waisted dress of royal blue crepe silk. Though the concierge had referred to her as "Madame" DuBois, Penelope saw no hint of a wedding ring, which made her all the more curious a figure.

Of course, that was the least of the things about

Madame DuBois that spurred Penelope's curiosity. "Finding" that wallet in the corridor had been awfully convenient. Though she had an instant dislike of Monsieur Barbier, Pen was inclined to believe him when he'd suggested this woman was a pickpocket. The only thing Penelope couldn't fathom was why. She certainly didn't seem like the typical petty thief, considering how well-made her dress was and the fact that she was in the First Class lounge area.

"I should be buying you that champagne, Madame DuBois," Lulu teased, knowing the drinks were free.

Madame DuBois laughed lightly, earning herself another round of nasty looks from Monsieur Barbier and his lovely companion. "Please, call me Honorine. Now then, I assume we are all off to Paris?"

"We are," Penelope answered. "Is that where you live?"

"But of course," Honorine said, smiling and lifting her champagne.

"And you were on the Côte d'Azur for...pleasure?"

Honorine squinted one eye at Penelope, a small smile playing on her lips. "*Non*."

Pen waited for her to expound until she realized no explanation would be forthcoming.

"It has been a pleasure. À bientôt!" Honorine said before Penelope could ask any more impertinent questions. She exited back to her sleeper carriage, glass of champagne in hand.

"Am I the only one who thinks that woman didn't just *happen* to find Monsieur Barbier's wallet?" Lulu asked.

"No, you aren't," Penelope said, watching Honorine disappear into the next car.

"She hardly seems like a woman who would need to steal," Benny said, then added in an impressed tone,

"That dress was Chanel, from this year's Spring Collection."

"Of course you'd know that," Lulu said, grinning at him, as though she wasn't just as hep to modern fashion.

"I'm sure we'd hear about it if the owner of that wallet had so much as a franc missing," Richard said, glancing back toward Monsieur Barbier, who was now smoking a cigarette and otherwise occupied with his coquette sitting across from him.

"So, what was she after?" Penelope wondered.

"I don't plan on making it any of my business. I've had enough adventure during this holiday, thank you very much," Lulu said.

"Yes, you're right of course," Pen said with a nod, turning her attention back to her friends. "No need to insert ourselves into another scandal. Tomorrow, we'll be in Paris and we can put this entire episode behind us."

"But first, we have to make it through dinner," Benny said with a devilish grin. "With our luck, we may find an even bigger scandal on our plates."

CHAPTER THREE

The stop in Cannes was just before the dinner service. Penelope and Richard had separated themselves from their friends to one of the duet tables in the lounge. She stared out the window to see who would be joining them on their short jaunt through France. The only additional First Class passenger was a man who seemed perfectly nondescript. He was perhaps in his fifties, with a slight build, wearing a gray suit and spectacles. He carried a single brown suitcase with him, turning down the offer of help from a young porter with an irritated shake of the head. He probably didn't want to tip for such a meager burden.

"Anyone interesting?" Richard said, his back to the scene.

"Not at all," Pen said with a sigh.

"Perhaps that's a good thing. I'd say we've had enough entertainment for the evening."

Penelope laughed and turned to look at Lulu, Benny, and Cousin Cordelia conspiring on the couch across from them. This trip had made the three of them thick as thieves.

Benny and Lulu were understandably aligned, both outsiders in their own way. Cousin Cordelia was the bigger surprise. Decades of prudence and old-fashioned sensibilities seemed to have gone right out the window. She didn't even bother referring to her occasional nips of brandy as "medicinal" anymore. Granted, Europe had yet to be afflicted by the bane that was Prohibition in the United States.

"We should get refreshed for dinner," Penelope said, finishing off her gimlet and rising from her chair.

"I'm feeling refreshed enough. I'll just wait here for you to return."

Penelope nodded and left, passing through the third and then the second carriages. Quentin was about to open the door to compartment 205 for the newest arrival on the train. Instead, they waited for her to pass. She smiled, but only Quentin returned one. The other man just seemed irritated by the delay.

She entered the passageway to get to the first carriage and could still smell the lingering scent of Lucien's cigarette. As she exited, she could hear the newest passenger tell Quentin that he had no need for his services during the trip, not even to turn down his bed. She turned to briefly look at him, mentally assessing him as a businessman who no doubt wanted to get some work done. Perhaps that was what his brown suitcase contained.

After a bit of freshening up in her room, Penelope returned to find she was the first to rejoin Richard, as the others had gone to their respective compartments to do the same. Lulu and Cousin Cordelia returned together and took the couch across from them again.

"It seems Benny is, once again, holding everyone up," Penelope groused as they watched the other First Class passengers from cars two and three file into the dining room. By the time Benny made a reappearance, Pen worried they wouldn't find a table to sit at together.

"Apologies, apologies," Benny sang, not sounding sorry at all for his tardiness. He had changed into a velvet-lined tuxedo jacket with a patterned burgundy ascot. "I wanted just the right wardrobe for dinner." He lifted his chin as though to direct everyone's eyes toward the silk paisley number at his neck.

"It's lovely, but I'm famished," Pen said, rising and leading them all into the dining room. It was separated from the lounge by a set of French doors, so one could see right into it.

As expected, it was nearly full. There were three rows of tables. On one side were tables for two and along the other side were tables for four. Each was laid with a crisp white tablecloth, fine table settings, and fresh flowers.

All the tables for two were taken. The man they'd had the disagreeable encounter with was already seated with his young companion at the furthest table. She had changed into a pretty pink silk dress for dinner. He was wearing the same expensive suit he'd had on earlier. He frowned at the newest arrivals then quickly averted his gaze to ignore them.

The next table was taken by the man who had boarded in Cannes. He sat by himself, facing Monsieur Barbier and his companion. Perhaps he enjoyed the view from behind of Cosette. Pen had to admit it presented a rather comely figure.

At the next table for two was a young couple, perhaps on their return from a honeymoon, considering their youthful appearance. The young blonde wife, who faced the entrance of the dining room, fiddled with her wedding ring as though unused to it on her finger. Penelope smiled knowingly at her as she entered, which caused one of her dark eyebrows to rise, as though surprised by the acknowledgment.

"There is only one table for four free," Cousin Cordelia lamented. "You two should sit together, Penelope, dear. Benny, Lulu, and I will be fine at a table to ourselves."

"Two lovely swans to accompany me at dinner? My cup runneth over," Benny crooned, instantly hooking each of his arms through Lulu's and Cousin Cordelia's. Lulu smirked while Penelope's cousin giggled like a girl as he escorted them a few feet to the middle table.

Penelope's eyes were drawn to the right side of the carriage. The middle table was the only one without any diners. Lucien sat at the furthest table, no doubt because it offered a perfect view of Cosette. He met Penelope's inadvertent gaze with one eyebrow suggestively arched, inviting her to join him.

"We'll take this table," Richard said, glaring at Lucien, then guiding Penelope to the nearest table. The two men who had mostly kept to themselves in the lounge during the earlier altercation were seated there.

"*Do you mind?*" Penelope asked one of the men in French, gesturing to the two free seats that were left at the third table. She was irked to see both of them already had their eyes settled on Richard, as though seeking his approval before the older one nodded and gestured for them to take the seats.

Richard was gracious enough to allow her the seat facing the rest of the dining car, including her friends sitting behind him. The two men didn't seem to be the talkative sort, even with each other. Pen had the idea she and Richard would be conversing only with themselves, which was fine by her.

The menus were instantly placed by an attentive waiter who also took their drink orders.

"It's quite the course selection for a simple overnight train voyage," Richard observed, looking at the options.

"As it should be, and there is nothing simple about this line. Only the Orient Express is a finer means of transportation through France."

They perused the selections and gave their orders to the waiter. Penelope was about to address the married couple across from them, who seemed more amenable to conversation. She was interrupted by the arrival of the final First Class passenger, once again making her entrance with élan.

"Ah, it seems I've arrived a bit late," Honorine said as she entered, drawing the attention of everyone in the room. Penelope couldn't help but think the woman had a flair for doing that. At the very least, her presence would make dinner a more interesting affair. Hopefully in a good way.

CHAPTER FOUR

Honorine looked around the dining room with an attractive frown as though deciding which table to choose. Her eyes briefly flicked to Lucien, alone at his table, and she understandably dismissed joining him. That left two options. The man in the gray suit seemed like a rather dull dinner companion, he didn't even enjoy a glass of wine with his meal, sticking to water. Benny, Lulu, and Cousin Cordelia had a spot free, and their expressions practically begged her to join them.

"It seems all the smaller tables are taken." Honorine smiled in a way that showed off a small dimple in her right cheek as she approached the table with Penelope's friends. "Do you mind terribly if I join you? I do hate eating alone."

"By all means," Benny was the first to quickly say. He gestured to the empty seat across from him next to Lulu, who seemed amused by the addition.

Penelope was also amused, mostly by the ease with which Honorine was able to ingratiate herself with others. She still wondered about that "missing" wallet. Perhaps the Chanel dress she wore was paid for via her occupation as a professional thief? Charm worked wonders as a distraction while one was picking a pocket.

As though reading her mind, Honorine tilted her head to the side so she could see past Richard, and shot Pen a knowing smile. "I'm awfully curious about your little group, but I suppose I should introduce myself first, no?"

"If you insist," Benny cheerily responded.

Penelope noted that even the couple at the table across from them seemed suddenly interested. Perhaps it was because she was situated at the middle table, literally positioning her at the center of attention. She'd managed to take Lucien's attention away from Cosette. The lone man across from her seemed mildly interested, though mostly in her shapely legs based on the direction of his eyes. Monsieur Barbier was understandably glaring at the back of her head, while Cosette casually glanced over her shoulder. The only two who didn't seem interested were the men sitting with Penelope and Richard. One stared out the window into the night and the other seemed preoccupied with his menu.

Honorine leaned in toward Benny conspiratorially and said in a breathy tone meant to mimic a whisper but loud enough for the entire dining room to hear, "I'm on a secret mission."

"Oh, do tell, dove," Benny crooned.

Honorine laughed and sat back in her seat. "To enjoy myself, of course. Monte Carlo is such a lovely place, even in the summer. Sadly, I lost more than a few francs while I was there. It is a good thing I am not a habitual gambler."

For some reason, Penelope didn't believe that either. She was good at reading people for bluffs, after years of gambling to make ends meet once upon a time. Now that she was a millionaire, thanks to an inheritance, those skills hadn't disappeared. Sadly, that specific talent didn't extend to the point that she knew exactly *what* someone was lying about.

A small, knowing smile appeared on Richard's face as he subtly moved his chair closer to the man next to him so Penelope wouldn't have to crane her neck to view the table behind him, particularly Honorine.

"You are traveling by yourself?" Cousin Cordelia asked.

Honorine put on a show of looking mildly offended. "I don't think it is frowned upon any longer, *non?*"

"No, I suppose not. Though, I did hear the concierge refer to you as Madame DuBois. I thought perhaps your husband had joined you."

"Ah yes, I can see why you must be confused. No, no, my husband is quite dead," Madame DuBois said cheerfully.

"I see," Cousin Cordelia said, despite sounding perfectly bewildered. Of course, Penelope's cousin had actually loved her dearly departed Harold. It seemed Honorine wasn't of a similar sentiment with her own deceased spouse.

Merry widow, indeed, Penelope thought to herself. She once again glanced at Richard, whose brow was lifted as high as hers was. Even the young woman across the aisle once again lifted her brow, this time in shock. While Honorine ordered her drink and course selections, Pen turned her attention to the couple.

"*Are you two newlyweds?*" Penelope asked in French.

The young man seemed surprised by the apparently intrusive question and quickly swiveled his head to frown at Penelope. The young woman grimaced, but quickly replaced it with a tight smile.

"*Yes, we're—*" She cast a quick, anxious look toward her husband as she fiddled even more with her ring.

"We're British," he finished for her, the switch to English and the accent confirming as much. That explained his wife's hesitancy. She probably wasn't fluent in French.

The conversation was momentarily interrupted by the gentleman in the grey suit, who stood and walked between them. Pen followed him with a small frown of irritation as he exited the car, then she turned her attention back to the couple.

"You must be here on your honeymoon?" Penelope asked, smiling as she switched to English for their benefit.

"Yes, we are," he said, a forced smile coming to his lips. His hand flashed across the table to take hold of his wife's. It might as well have been a snake biting her for how much it made her start in surprise. Still, she offered a grateful smile, as though happy he was there to field such apparently sticky questions as the status of their relationship and reason for traveling.

"Yes, that's right, we're on our honeymoon," the young woman parroted, now seemingly much more at ease. Her smile was more natural and relaxed, and she slipped her hand out of her husband's to take hold of her water. "Just back from—"

"Menton," her husband interrupted, once again finishing for her. It hardly seemed necessary at that point. Penelope certainly hoped his new wife would do something about that if she planned on spending the rest of her life with him.

"And the two of you?" His eyes slipped down to Penelope's left hand with her engagement ring. "Your reason for traveling?"

Penelope sensed an undertone of impertinence, as though swatting her intrusiveness right back at her. Two perfectly innocent questions hardly seemed an interrogation. Still, she was congenial in her tone when she answered. "We're all on holiday, the five of us. Richard and I aren't married yet."

"Engaged," Richard said, shooting her a smile. Penelope smiled back and held up her hand with the ring on it. It was a gray pearl abutted by two jade stones.

"How lovely," the young woman said, gazing at the ring with something approaching longing. There was only the solitary, thin gold band on her finger, which was hardly unusual. Better to spend that money on a lovely First Class trip to the French Riviera. Penelope was flattered Richard had even thought to get her a ring to propose, though any plans for a wedding had yet to be discussed. They had time.

The woman continued to stare at Penelope's ring. "When is your wedding?"

"I'm sure they don't want to chat with perfect strangers," her husband hinted in a curt tone. When she showed no signs of returning her attention to him, he added for emphasis, "*Marie.*"

Marie's head snapped back to face him "Yes, of course... Thomas."

She didn't seem chagrined or embarrassed. Penelope supposed he had already "tamed" her into obeying his commands, just like a trained poodle. Penelope was poised to resume conversing just to defy him. Richard cleared his throat pointedly, giving her a look that all but told her she couldn't solve every problem. After all, if Marie's husband was a bully, he'd still be one with or without Pen's help.

If Penelope had any intention of following through with her plans, despite that, they were interrupted by the arrival of the soup course. More to the point, they were interrupted by one diner's accident with said course.

Monsieur Barbier shouted a curse in French before

continuing into a rant. "*Look at this, potage all over my jacket! See what you have caused, Cosette?*"

Pen shifted her attention to that table to see him throw his napkin down and shoot up from his chair. He glared at the rest of the dining car, who had directed their attention toward him after his outburst. There was a stain on the jacket that he quickly removed. Fortunately for him, it hadn't touched the white dress shirt underneath. He stormed out of the car, moving so quickly, Pen felt a small breeze in his wake.

"*If he fails to return, I shall be happy to keep you company over dinner,*" Lucien crooned to Cosette. Penelope couldn't see him from her vantage point, now that she was no longer craning her neck. However, the withering look Cosette gave him was enough to reveal her unspoken answer. Pen heard him laugh in response.

"Quite the entertainment while we dine, *non?*" Honorine said with a cheerful little laugh. Pen watched her lean in toward her dinner companions and add, "I know which dinner companion I would prefer."

Lucien, having easily heard that, laughed even heartier. Cosette made a soft sound of irritation and rose from her seat to escape the dining room as well. She glared once at Lucien, then at the back of Honorine's head before she passed. Perhaps Penelope had misjudged her role. Usually, a kept woman, especially a French one, wouldn't have been so priggish.

Coincidentally, Penelope did note Richard's eyes follow Cosette. It seemed the man in the gray suit wasn't the only one who admired the back of her. She smirked and arched a brow. "I was just about to sympathize with you having your back turned to the entertainment, but it seems you're enjoying a show of your own."

Richard smiled and breathed out a laugh, dutifully returning his attention to his fiancée. "I have managed to grasp the gist of it all. Besides, there's presently enough of a show in my line of sight."

That had Penelope curious enough to turn her head to look over her shoulder. She was just in time to catch Cosette doing an awkward dance with Mr. Gray Suit as they navigated going different directions through the door leading to the passageway between cars. Cosette looked exasperated. Mr. Gray Suit seemed to be deliberately making it more challenging if only to brush up against her a bit more. The indignant look on her face as she cast one last look his way, and the subtle smile on his as he finally made his way past her had Penelope suspecting that was indeed the case. That made him even more dull and disappointing than Pen had first assumed.

"I'm disappointed you find such a show so amusing," Pen said, a scornful tone to her voice as she turned her attention back to Richard.

"More interesting than amusing."

"How so?" Pen asked, suddenly intrigued.

"I don't think everything is quite as it seems on this train."

CHAPTER FIVE

Richard's words had more than a few heads turned his way. Considering how small the dining area was, that wasn't a surprise. Even the two men seated at the same table as Penelope and Richard had finally taken an interest in something other than the menu or the view out of the window.

"What do you mean things aren't quite what they seem?" Penelope asked.

"I think we'd all like to know," Honorine said behind him.

Richard seemed to regret having said anything in the first place. Though, he did raise his eyebrows in a meaningful way, as though the woman who had just spoken was exhibit A in the court of things that were not what they seemed on board the train. He judiciously kept that to himself. "I suppose it's just a feeling."

"Odd, I have the same feeling," Honorine mused a hint of taunting in her voice. Now, Penelope was sure she knew everyone suspected her of having stolen Monsieur Barbier's wallet. Though, it had to be asked, why didn't she care?

Penelope turned to the two men, who had cast a few surreptitious glances at each other during this exchange. There was some definite unspoken communication happening between them.

"What do you two gentlemen think? Is there some subterfuge occurring right underneath our noses?" She had spoken English as they had both reacted to Richard's announcement spoken in that language. Her voice was girlish and playful, the kind of tone meant to lower the defenses of men. Neither seemed swayed by it.

The younger one sitting next to Richard, cast a look his way. Again, Penelope felt her bristles flutter as it seemed he was questioning why Richard couldn't keep her from speaking out of turn. It made her want to be even more audacious.

She made her tone even more teasing when she continued. "Perhaps you are involved in a bit of subterfuge of your own?"

"What are you implying?" The younger man was defensive. He had a French accent, but his English was perfectly passable.

"*André, she is simply teasing us,*" his older traveling partner admonished. He turned to Penelope with an apologetic smile and switched to English. "Pardon my friend. He is weary from traveling."

"Yes, it can be tiring, even in such luxurious accommodations." She left the sardonic tone out of her voice, allowing them to interpret her meaning however they wished. If one had to travel, First Class on this train in particular would hardly leave one exhausted. She wondered what they had been involved in prior to boarding. Now that she was seated closer to them, she noted the tell-tale signs that their suits were not tailored or made to fit. Whatever the French version of the Sears catalog was, they had very likely been purchased from it. Yes, purchased at the higher end—they had at least made an attempt to appear like they belonged in First Class. She turned her attention to the more amenable man sitting next to her. "Are you heading to Paris as well?"

"But of course," he said with a smile. "It is home, you see. André and I were visiting a friend in Menton."

"How nice for your friend, living in such a lovely city—and nice for you to have a reason to visit."

"Certainly a nice holiday from selling insurance," he said in a jovial tone. "I am Simon Pougnet and my friend here is André Robineau."

Monsieur Robineau didn't seem pleased by the introductions, but managed to flash a quick smile Penelope's way. He then pointedly turned to look out the window.

"Are you two on holiday as well?"

"Yes," Richard answered. "Heading to Paris after several months in Antibes."

"Ah, another one of our country's beautiful cities on the Mediterranean. Paris is lovely as well, of course. Have you visited before?"

"After the war. In fact, I will be visiting a few fellow former soldiers, several of whom have decided to call Paris home."

"Yes, yes, the war; terrible business." Simon shook his head with a woeful expression. His face softened and he turned to Penelope. "And you, mademoiselle?"

"I have, also after the war. I mostly dallied with artists and poets," she cast a quick, impish smile Richard's way, "though I suppose that doesn't discount their being former soldiers. That intersection is inevitable for young men of a certain age."

"*Oui, oui*, I know far too many of them, I'm afraid. Some who didn't make it back."

"Not to mention the devastation to our country," André added, his interest in the conversation suddenly igniting some passion in him. "Certain people have seen fit to profit unjustly."

"Oh?" Now, Penelope was the one whose interest had been piqued.

Simon chuckled, or perhaps cleared his throat in a jovial manner. Though, she did note him giving his friend another censuring look. "Such is often the case with war."

"Indeed. Though I hate to think of any of my fellow compatriots contributing to it," Richard said, casting a somber look at each man.

"Ah, it seems our next course has arrived," Simon said, looking past him. Penelope had the distinct impression he wanted to change the topic, or at least divert their attention. This was bolstered by the intense look that passed between the two men as Richard briefly turned his head.

Luckily for them, another head-turner arrived that was even more enticing than the dish presently being served at the furthest tables. A wave of flowing, pink silk, capped by a crop of blonde hair breezed past. There was also the lingering scent of something floral and exotic in Cosette's wake.

Across the aisle, Pen noted Marie's dark eyes pinned on Cosette, turning her head to follow her to the table. The expression on her face resembled that of a child being forced to eat a disagreeable vegetable. It seemed the new bride disapproved of the other woman's less formal relationship with Monsieur Barbier. She reached up to pat her own blonde hair, less perfectly coifed in a longer cut, held back on one side with a similar trio of bobby pins. Her hands then fell to smooth down the skirt of her dress, which was nice and expensive, but at a length that had gone out of fashion several years earlier. Pen supposed not every woman wanted to bare their knees in public, though prudishness seemed odd for a woman so young. However, it didn't seem to carry to her makeup, which boasted the kind of vibrant reddish coloring on both her cheeks and lips at which Penelope's father would have wagged his finger. It wasn't especially garish, but it had that effect as it was applied with a heavy, inexperienced hand. Perhaps her new husband—who certainly had his eyes trained hard on Cosette's retreating figure, almost to the point of ferocity—demanded it of his wife.

Quentin arrived a few steps behind her, and they approached the waiter, then paused to briefly converse.

"*Monsieur Barbier will be taking the rest of his dinner in his quarters. Please coordinate with Quentin to have that taken care of,*" Cosette said to the waiter. She then turned to Quentin. "*Be sure to leave it outside his door, as he does not wish to be disturbed. Simply knock once and announce that the dinner has arrived.*"

Cosette took her seat at the table, and Quentin continued on to the kitchen.

"*I sense an opportunity is afoot. It seems you are without company for the rest of the evening, mademoiselle,*" Lucien said, his voice dripping with suggestion.

"*Then your senses are as insolent and unwelcome as you are,* monsieur."

Lucien's response to this chilly retort was to laugh yet again. He was obviously the rakish sort who was no doubt quite used to such rebuffs from women.

The waiter had reached their table and was serving each person the meal they had requested. When he had finished and departed to the kitchen, Penelope picked up her fork to eat. The potage had been delicious but she was still quite famished. This voyage to Europe had done something awful to her appetite. At this rate, she'd probably have to go clothes shopping in Paris out of necessity rather than desire. Before she could even take a bite of her main course, her attention was snatched away by the abrupt motion next to her.

"I need something from my cabin," Marie's husband announced. He stood from his seat and quickly left through the lounge area to exit the carriage.

"Thomas, wait!"

Rather than wait for an answer, Marie also got up and quickly left, following him. Penelope looked after them over her shoulder. Marie caught up with Thomas in the tiny passageway between the carriages. There was a brief argument before Thomas shook his head and continued on, a resigned Marie following him.

"How odd." Penelope turned back to Richard, quite puzzled.

"Yes, it was," André answered instead, suspicion coloring both his tone and facial expression as he looked past Penelope to the exit.

"Not any business of ours," Simon said. He made an attempt to sound dismissive of it, but Pen noted the way he gave a pointed look to his friend.

"Yes, very odd indeed," Richard said. His focus was on his plate as he said it, but his eyes rolled up to meet Penelope's as though to say "I told you so."

CHAPTER SIX

The rest of dinner proceeded without much fanfare. Quentin reappeared with the remaining courses of Monsieur Barbier's dinner on a tray. He stopped to collect his drink from the table and continued on to deliver the service.

Marie and Thomas returned not long after that. They seemed more sedate as they entered the dining area, Marie hugging his arm with both of hers, guiding him like a patient mother with a temperamental child. Everyone at the table across from them watched, hoping to glean what Thomas's exodus was truly about. They revealed nothing, and in fact, didn't even seem interested in each other. They quietly ate and drank, seemingly lost in their own thoughts, though Marie did cast the occasional worried glance Thomas's way. Perhaps she was concerned about another abrupt departure.

The man in the gray suit was happily enjoying his own meal, ignoring everyone else. Though her back was to Penelope, Cosette was doing the same to Lucien, who had finally paid heed to her suggestion that she had no interest in him.

As for Penelope, she was now perfectly in agreement

with Richard, things certainly weren't what they seemed on board the train. The two fellows next to them had reverted to their recalcitrant, unsociable selves, focusing only on their food and the scenery. The train was still going along the coast, but their view was toward land, so there was little of interest to see, if one could actually see anything at all in the darkness. Any attempts at conversation on Penelope's part were met with terse responses or simple nods.

The occupants of the table behind Richard had no such problem as they continued to gaily laugh and chat. Multiple orders of drinks had helped with that. Penelope enjoyed listening to the conversation second-hand as she devoured her meal to an almost embarrassing degree. She reassured herself that she would be more restrained once she reached England, their last stop before returning to New York. Paris was certainly no city in which to practice restraint. This was evidenced by the stories with which Honorine regaled her table mates.

"It was an absolute delight. The Eiffel Tower was painted gold for the Exhibition. I had to sneak away to attend, you know. I was a young widow at the time, married to a much older man. In those years, widows had to remain in mourning for a year!"

"You attended while in mourning?" Cousin Cordelia was perfectly scandalized.

"A marriage of convenience is hardly convenient if one must miss the fair of the century, no?" Honorine laughed lightly, and Benny and Lulu joined her. Penelope could imagine Cousin Cordelia's invisible pearls still clutched in her hand.

"At any rate, I was quite fascinated by the American's exhibition. Monsieur W.E.B. Du Bois—though the gentleman running the exhibit both spelled and pronounced it incorrectly, if I must say so; such is the American way!—had a fascinating display. It was titled The American Negro. And the food? My favorite were the little pancakes made of cornmeal—Johnny cakes they called them."

"I hope they at least served it with molasses," Lulu said.

"Oh yes! Yet another fascination. Most of the French shied away, as it was all corn, you see. Even the food prepared by the gourmet chef could not tempt them. As a staple usually reserved for peasants, I must say, the food they prepared was quite delicious. I wouldn't have bothered if not for the encouragement of a young woman I saw. In fact..."

Penelope blinked in surprise mid-bite as Honorine leaned sideways to look past Benny to consider her. "Hmm," she hummed with a knowing smile before sitting straight again, out of Penelope's line of sight. "It wasn't long after that when I was arrested, first for theft, and then for *murder*."

That, naturally, had the entire table astir. In fact, most of the people in the dining room seemed to have taken notice. One of Richard's eyebrows quirked up as he met Penelope's gaze. André next to him turned his head to view Honorine, while Simon craned his neck. Marie's eyes went wide as her head swiveled around so she could gape at Honorine, before quickly turning back to her own meal in embarrassment at the naked reaction. However, Thomas's frown remained directed that way. Even Mr. Gray Suit sported a bemused smile as he turned to observe her. Only Cosette seemed uninterested, her back and head studiously facing the rest of the dining car. Penelope couldn't see Lucian's reaction, but she heard his soft chuckle.

Honorine laughed in a tinkling, impish manner. "I was

innocent, of course—of both crimes mind you. In fact, it was a rather handsome devil of a man who—oh, but I am monopolizing the conversation. Please, tell me of your adventures in Antibes."

"Don't you dare!" Benny scolded. "You must continue. Do tell us about this handsome devil you met."

Honorine laughed yet again. "Perhaps once I return. I do believe all this wine has affected me. If you'll excuse me."

Penelope almost admired her ability to hold an audience hostage in such a devilish manner. Even she had to admit, she was enthralled with the idea of their most interesting fellow passenger being accused of both theft and murder. However, her innocence back then certainly didn't negate it presently. Pen was still certain Monsieur Barbier's wallet had been stolen, not "found."

"I must say, she is quite the fascinating woman," Lucien said to no one in particular. "A young widow, then accused of murder, and now here on board with us. Should we be worried?"

"Why don't you excuse yourself to go and molest *her* with your pestering and taunting," Cosette snipped.

That only had the easily amused Lucien laughing again. "Perhaps I shall. At the very least to make sure Monsieur Barbier does not suffer another loss of his wallet." He rose and strolled out of the dining room into the lounge and bar area.

Pen turned to see him escape into the next car, then turned back to smile down at her plate as she forked another bite of her fish. "I do hope that fellow doesn't do anything untoward with Madame DuBois."

"That Miss DuBois is one lady who can take care of herself," Lulu said, a wry smile on her face that Penelope could see between Richard and André.

"I dare say, she might very well indulge in a bit of something untoward with him," Benny said in a suggestive voice. "He is rather daring to look at and a fine dresser. I suppose we'll know, depending on how wrinkled that dress of hers is when she returns."

"Oh, *Benny*," Cousin Cordelia scolded, though she did manage a slight giggle.

The waiter came by to take their finished entrées. Penelope was still craving more, and looked forward to dessert. Not so, her fellow guests at the table.

"We will be skipping dessert, if you'll excuse us," Simon said, eyeing his partner in a meaningful way.

André looked surprised at first, then disappointed, and finally resigned. He nodded and rose along with his friend. Penelope watched them leave, in wonder. It was one thing to pass on dessert if one was trying to avoid indulging too much. She could see how perhaps Simon, who was both older and heavier than his friend, might refrain. However, André was, if anything, too thin. She eyed Richard who watched their retreating figures with interest.

"There are two men with something to hide," she suggested.

"Hmm?" Richard returned his distracted attention back to her questioningly.

"Don't you think their behavior has been odd tonight?"

"I think they just aren't very sociable."

"Really?" He'd been so quick to label others' behavior as suspicious, but seemed to see nothing wrong with two men who were all too eager to avoid conversation or even dessert—which, if it was as good as dinner was, promised to be delicious. Perhaps as a man, he better understood their behavior. Penelope dismissed it in favor of the crème brûlée she had chosen. Yes, she really would have to temper her growing appetite before returning to New York.

Honorine returned, dress decidedly unwrinkled. "Ah, I see my cheese plate has arrived ahead of me. Just in time for a bit more wine," she gave the waiter an arched eyebrow by way of making her request. He instantly jumped to get more for her.

"And just in time to tell us about this handsome devil from the Paris Exhibition?" Benny hinted.

"Ah yes, well, as it turns out..." She continued and Penelope listened. The story was almost as fascinating as her crème brûlée was delicious. It seemed the adventure Miss DuBois had experienced twenty-six years ago made up for the lack of one she had with Monsieur Vollant. That made Penelope wonder what he had gotten himself up to now that Honorine was back.

When he did return, he drifted in on a scent of strong tobacco, which explained what he'd been up to. Penelope did note that there was no exchange of glances between Honorine and him. In fact, Honorine seemed overly entranced by Cousin Cordelia's retelling of her own adventures at the 1889 Paris Exhibition. Though, there was no murder or theft to add any excitement. Either Honorine was a very considerate listener, or she didn't want to invite any supposition about goings on between Lucien and her. Or perhaps Penelope was simply reading too much into everything that had happened over dinner.

CHAPTER SEVEN

Thomas was the first to stand up to leave after finishing his dessert.

"Are you coming, Marie?"

"No, I'd...like to sit for a while," she said. He stared at her for a moment, as though waiting for her to change her mind, then sighed and left alone. When he was gone, she got up to take his seat, and stared at the back of Cosette as though studying a painting. She idly patted her blonde hair, straightening both bobby pins, perhaps considering a new shade or cut to match the far more fashionable and modern Cosette.

"Merci beaucoup, for allowing me to dine with you. It has been a pleasure!" Honorine announced, standing up to leave. As she exited, she met Penelope with an enigmatic smile and a nod. Penelope wondered what had Madame DuBois taking such a particular interest in her. She turned to watch her leave.

In her periphery, she noted Marie sit up a bit straighter, as though something had caught her attention. Penelope turned her head back around to see Lucien had risen from

43

his seat and was now leaning over, whispering to Cosette. The teasing smile on his lips gave every indication as to what he was saying. Penelope felt a stab of sympathy for her. It was not easy being a beautiful woman, even if one did use that beauty to her advantage with men. It still welcomed so much unwanted attention from the wrong sort. Cosette, to her credit, remained sitting with her shoulders set, not that she seemed like the wilting flower type.

Lucien pulled away from Cosette's ear with a satisfied smile on his face. He noted the way Marie stared at him, wide-eyed, and winked at her. Penelope caught her violently blush and an expression of self-castigation came to her face, no doubt reminding herself of her married status. As though underlining that admonishment, she began fiddling with her ring once again.

Penelope heard Cosette exhale either in anger or frustration before she threw her napkin on the table and stormed out in a huff. Marie watched her every step, waiting until Cosette had passed through the lounge and into the next car before she stood to leave herself.

The man in the gray suit was the last of the others to depart the dining room. He took the last leisurely bite of his dessert, leaned back with a satisfied sigh, then stood. He offered a mild smile and a nod to the only remaining passengers, Penelope and her friends, as he left.

"Now there was a mass exodus that could shame even Moses's dramatic endeavor," Benny mused.

"Don't be blasphemous, Benjamin," Cousin Cordelia scolded.

"He does have a point," Lulu said. "There is more to this story than what we're seeing on the page, if you catch my drift."

"Richard, you thought there was something odd

happening," Penelope said, rising to take the seat the man in the gray suit had just vacated. Richard rose to take the other, so they could both face the other three.

"It's probably harmless. A cad, a coquette, a married couple, and several otherwise ordinary men."

"And Honorine DuBois," Penelope added.

"She was a delight. I can't imagine her harboring any ill intention," Cousin Cordelia championed. "She was the one to find that man's wallet, after all, and she returned it with nothing stolen."

There was no point in arguing with her cousin, who seemed to have made her mind up about the woman. Penelope, however, knew a bit too much about putting on a deceptive performance. Poker had taught her how to bluff like an expert.

The waiter came out and gave them all questioning looks. "Would you like coffee or a digestif? Perhaps something else to eat?"

"Nothing for me," Penelope said, feeling the meal and drinks begin to have an effect on her. "It was delicious, thank you."

She rose to leave and Richard joined her. The others lingered, each ordering a drink before leaving. Lucien was in the lounge, smoking a cigarette and enjoying an after-dinner digestif. His brow was wrinkled, as though he was deep in thought. Whatever it was that was on his mind was such that he didn't even notice Penelope and Richard passing by him.

The older concierge, whose name Pen still didn't know, was just entering the lounge car as they were about to exit. He dutifully held the door open for them to enter the passageway, then hurried on into the lounge. In the second car, Pen saw that the concierge's chair was also empty.

Having seen him as they passed through on their way to dinner, she knew that was Quentin's carriage. Perhaps he was in one of the compartments turning down the bed. However, the car seemed eerily silent, as though each occupant was listening and waiting for Penelope and Richard to pass through. She wondered which passengers were housed in that car.

She turned to meet Richard's eye and he seemed to have the same odd sensation. The silence had them doing the same, remaining quiet as mice during their progression along the corridor in the hopes that even a cough or rustle of sheets might hint at signs of life. However, the silence remained.

Halfway down that carriage, Penelope noted the lingering scent of cigarette smoke, which grew stronger as they neared the exit door. It was much stronger in the passageway. Pen wrinkled her nose with distaste as her eyes began to water. She didn't know why she was so sensitive to smells lately, and found certain ones particularly offensive. Only a few years ago, she had spent nights playing cards in backrooms so thick with cigarette smoke you could hardly see. It hadn't bothered her much then, other than how easily it clung to one's clothing and hair. Sadly, the smell seemed to have carried into their car.

"Good evening, Monsieur, Mademoiselle. "I hope the meal was to your liking?" Jules greeted. He was setting down the silver bucket with an open bottle of champagne at his station. Someone in the other car must have requested a glass. He quickly walked over to greet them, and she could smell the scent of cigarettes on him. That confirmed he'd had to go through the smokey passageway to another car to serve the champagne in Quentin's absence.

"It was delicious," she said, hurrying past him.

"Very good. I have turned down your beds for the evening. Again, if you need anything, I will be right here."

She certainly hoped he'd turned down her bed before Lucien had taken his break for a cigarette in their passageway. Once she was further away, she turned to pose a question. "How many passengers are there in that second carriage?"

"It is fully booked, Mademoiselle." Jules gave her a questioning look.

Penelope smiled at how silly the question must have seemed. Silence was often a good sign, particularly that late at night. Perhaps they too had succumbed to a full meal and too much wine, and were happily asleep. She didn't bother with the follow-up question about where Quentin might have been at the moment. All that nonsense about their fellow passengers hiding something was obviously playing with her imagination. Tomorrow, they would be in Paris and all would be fine. Of course, they still had the rest of the night. She turned to grin at Richard, who was obviously thinking the same thing. All thoughts of their fellow passengers disappeared.

CHAPTER EIGHT

Richard and Penelope said goodnight to Jules and entered their respective compartments. The beds had been turned down, but blessedly, Pen's didn't have any lingering odors of cigarettes. She began changing out of her dress. After refreshing herself in the toilet and changing into her night clothes, she smiled and opened her door that led to the next compartment. She knocked on Richard's door and waited.

"Should I play the same game of asking who it is?" Richard said with teasing mirth in his voice.

"If you're expecting anyone other than Penelope Banks, I have to rethink this ring on my finger."

He laughed and opened his own door. She found him already in his pajamas. "Your cabin or mine?"

"You should come into mine as it's the last one. I wouldn't want to wake the neighbors with our misadventures," she replied with a grin.

He laughed again, then entered her compartment. For some awful reason, the dinner came rushing back to Pen's brain, and she couldn't let go of it. The odd silence from the next car, as well as the missing Quentin, had her mind filled with anything but romance.

"What do you believe is so odd about our fellow First Class passengers?" Penelope asked, draping her arms around his neck.

He arched an eyebrow. "Is that really what you want to talk about at the moment?"

"It's just that I had the same odd sense something more is going on. Perhaps not nefarious but...something. Take the gentlemen at our table. I know you didn't find their behavior strange, but I think there is more to them than simple reticence."

"Oh, I'm sure they are harmless. I had a chance to speak with them before you and Benny boarded the train...finally. I was first on board from our group and the bar was already open, so I indulged. They're just two simple men who I'm sure were visiting a friend as they claimed."

"And just happened to travel First Class? Did you note their clothes? Not to sound like a perfect snob, but the tickets must have been quite the splurge for them. They didn't even eat dessert!"

Richard frowned as he looked down at her. "You really are observant."

"You're just now learning that?" She shot him a teasing smile.

"Who else did you happen to observe with such an acute eye?"

"Everyone, really. I suspect the Widow DuBois stole that wallet."

"I don't think you're alone in that assessment," Richard said with a laugh.

"And the couple across from us. For being on their honeymoon, they're awfully unromantic with one another."

"Perhaps this marriage wasn't their choice. Or perhaps they don't feel it's necessary to advertise their passion."

"And that Cosette. I can't quite put my finger on what was wrong with that picture. As for Lucien? Well, he's nothing more than a Lothario, I suppose."

"My dear, we have one night on this train. We've also had enough suspicious activity on this grand voyage to Europe to satisfy both our occupations as investigators. Let's not invite trouble where it doesn't yet exist."

Penelope sighed, then shot him a devilish grin. "I suppose you're right. In fact, I can think of a different kind of trouble we can invite."

"Just the kind of trouble I like." Richard leaned down to kiss her, and Penelope once again forgot all about their fellow passengers.

Later, when Richard had retired back to his own quarters, Penelope was startled out of her sleep by a sound. She sat up in bed, wondering what it could be. Before she could turn on the lamp to look at her watch, she felt the train begin to slow down. It took her a moment to remember that there was a stop in Marseilles scheduled for just after midnight. The lights of the station that glowed through the gap in the curtains confirmed as much.

Rather than get her watch, she simply opened them to peek out at the passengers that boarded or disembarked, if any. Considering the time, it was understandable how abandoned the station was. Even traveling on one of the finest trains in France, it was a lot to ask for someone to board a half hour after midnight. Still, she did note some luggage being taken off. The brown suitcase she'd seen Mr. Gray

Suit carry on board was carried by a young porter. She smiled at the poor boy, who probably didn't get much in the way of tips having to work this odd shift. She had a feeling Mr. Gray Suit wasn't the generous type when it came to tipping. Pen took a moment to admire the young man, the lean muscles of his physique nicely outlined in his uniform as he set the suitcase onto a trolley. Laughing to herself, she closed the curtain just as she saw Quentin disembark to hand him a slip of paper and say something to him. It seemed there was only one passenger departing or boarding, and the least interesting one to boot. From Cannes to Marseilles, such a short trip to take so late at night. Perhaps Mr. Gray Suit had urgent business to take care of.

Now that she had been awakened, Pen found she couldn't get back to sleep. This wasn't unusual lately. Her sleep hadn't been very regular during most of this trip to Europe. There were times in the middle of the day when she was perfectly exhausted, only to find herself quite restless in the middle of the night. Unfortunately, that night, or rather, early morning, she found her restlessness more pronounced than usual. Perhaps it was the cabin itself. As spacious as it was, it still felt rather stuffy.

She turned on the lamp and grabbed her book. It was a mystery by Abner Ellis, whom Penelope knew by his real name thanks to a prior case. Considering how astute he'd been in helping her solve that mystery, it was no wonder she was enjoying the book. Even with such an engrossing book, she had no interest in sitting up in bed to read. The train was set to arrive in Paris at 2:20 in the afternoon, with only one stop in Lyon at a little after six in the morning.

Penelope sighed, then quickly swiveled to swing her legs off the side of the bed. There was all-night bar service, perhaps she would have some company if she departed to the lounge area. At the very least, she'd have more space in which to enjoy her book.

After debating simply throwing on her kimono and risking the scandal of publicly reading in such a state of dress, Pen shook her head and laughed. She had been more daring than that before, but only in a pinch. Instead, she changed into proper clothing. She had only the next day's dress to wear, so she donned that, then dabbed a bit of makeup on, just in case she wasn't alone in the lounge. She grabbed her book and exited her cabin.

Jules instantly became alert, rising from his seat at her appearance. "Did you need something, Mademoiselle Banks?"

She smiled and shook her head. "Just suffering a bit of insomnia. I'm going to the lounge."

"Very well," he said, returning a smile.

She continued past him into the second car. She caught Quentin returning from the platform, and smiled by way of greeting. He smiled and nodded as he took his seat while she passed into the third car. She smiled and nodded again to the third concierge before proceeding into the lounge and dining car. Pen steadied herself as she heard the whistle sound, declaring the last call to board before the train continued its voyage.

As she walked through the passage into the next car, she didn't see anyone seated at first and she assumed she was alone. Her eyes trailed further down and noted two figures conversing in the empty dining area. The lights were off in that part of the car, so she couldn't tell who they were. Their proximity to one another was quite intimate, though it looked as though they were arguing rather than indulging in a bit of romance. The French doors were closed, so they probably didn't hear her enter, and Pen wondered if she should announce herself in some manner. Of course, there was a bartender on duty, so it wasn't as though they had any expectation of full privacy. As she moved closer, she found herself rather surprised upon discovering who the two individuals were.

CHAPTER NINE

Penelope felt the train begin to move, which stirred her into opening the door to enter the bar area. The bartender seemed glad of the company, but Penelope's gaze was still locked on the scene before her through the French doors leading to the dining room.

"May I get you something, Mademoiselle?"

Penelope tore her eyes away from the couple arguing and to the bartender. Only the offer of a drink—and yes, the tactlessness of being so nosy—could snatch her attention away.

"I, er, yes, I suppose a drink would be nice. It may even help me get back to sleep. Just a gin and tonic, if you please." He smiled, nodded, and got to work making her drink, and Penelope turned her attention back to the couple.

Now that she was a bit closer and had taken a longer look, the man was quite obviously Lucien. No other man in First Class cut quite that tall and debonaire a figure. At first, Pen thought it was Cosette with him. That was until she saw the length of the blonde hair as well as the hemline of the dress she was still wearing. It was Marie, which was surprising. Penelope hadn't seen the two interact at all during dinner, other than Lucien's usual fare of rakish behavior. Then, of course, there was Marie's marital status. Whatever she was saying to Lucien, she was quite passionate about it. Certainly something more than an inappropriate comment or a suggestive solicitation on his part. As for Lucien, his demeanor of nonchalance had been replaced by one of silent intensity, as though he was giving Marie a warning look with nothing more than a hard stare.

Penelope decided she would press the bartender for a bit of information, while she had him, if only to satisfy her curiosity. "That couple in there, how long have they been, ah, talking?"

"Talking?" One side of his mouth hitched up and he met her with a sardonic gaze.

"Arguing," she corrected with a small laugh, turning her attention back to them. "What happened?"

"She was already here with a club soda. Then, Monsieur arrived, ordered a drink, and took the table across from her. This was perhaps ten minutes ago. They ignored each other, though I could see him eyeing her. I assumed he was interested. She was not." That quirk of his mouth happened again as he recalled it. "He was quite bold, I must say. After all, she is a married woman, no? He moved to join her. I did not hear what was said, but I saw her reaction." He laughed softly, which was enough of an explanation.

"She didn't get up and leave, or go to another chair?"

The bartender shook his head as he handed Penelope her glass. "But she did make her feelings on the matter known. Again, I only heard portions of it. 'How dare you.' 'You have no right.' Words such as that. It was in English."

Penelope nodded and pointed to the dining room. "How did they end up in there?"

"I believe he was the one to suggest it. I have the feeling they did not want me to overhear."

Penelope turned to look at the two once again. It seemed her observance had triggered their attention. They both stared at her, neither happy at having an audience. Marie looked alarmed, which was understandable. Lucien looked irritated, which was a surprise. He certainly hadn't bothered to hide his Casanova behavior before then.

Marie was the first to break away. She stormed back into the lounge area and practically fled through to the third car, casting only one quick, panicked glance Penelope's way. Lucien remained in the dining room, staring after her with a thoughtful expression, as though mentally evaluating their heated exchange. He pulled out a pack of cigarettes and stuck one into his mouth. It was only then that he shifted his attention to Penelope, grinning around the stick and winking at her. She busied herself with her drink, hoping he wouldn't shift his unwanted attention to her. She was set to retreat to one of the armchairs when she noted him patting the pockets of his jacket with a frustrated expression, apparently missing his lighter. He gave up and headed toward the lounge area. Penelope quickly escaped to a corner and sat in one of the armchairs with her drink and her book. Fortunately, he approached the bar instead and addressed the bartender.

"I am afraid I must request another box of matches. I left the last box in my compartment."

"Of course, Monsieur." The bartender reached underneath the bar and pulled out a small box of matches to give to him. The box was the same dark blue as the train, with gold lettering advertising the line. Penelope easily translated

the exchange, thinking back to the attractive lighter Lucien had used earlier. It was a shame if it was indeed lost, as it seemed expensive. The annoyed look on his face as he pulled out a match and lit his cigarette told her it was quite valuable to him.

Lucien saw her observing him and held up the box. "Free advertising for the company. I would admire their ingenuity, but it's rather inconvenient having to resort to matches rather than a lighter. Mine seems to have gone missing."

"A shame, It was a handsome piece."

He hummed in disgruntled agreement as he took a drag, then blew it out. He walked over and boldly took the chair across from her. "I see I'm not the only one who prefers the night hours."

"I simply couldn't sleep." She opened her book by way of a hint.

"Perhaps you would like me to help with that?" He grinned around his cigarette.

"Really, *Monsieur*, that is quite inappropriate. And if you don't mind, I would rather you didn't smoke near me, as I'm quite sensitive to it."

He laughed, but held his cigarette further away from her. "I did not mean it that way." He gave her a daring look. "Unless of course you are open to it. Not to worry, my lips know when to remain closed...or open as necessary." He again laughed at her indignation.

"I'm engaged."

"That has never been an obstacle for *moi*."

"I'm sure it hasn't. It is, however, one for me. Even if I weren't, I wouldn't be so inclined."

"And after I've offered to be so generous with my affections." He pouted with disingenuous offense.

"Perhaps Marie wasn't enough to warn you how undesirable your affections are?"

"Madame *Smith*?" A cryptic smile came to his face. "She is not quite the innocent new wife she claims to be."

"Oh?" Penelope found her curiosity overshadowing her desire to be left alone.

"Oh," was his only blunt response. He looked off to the side in thought for a brief moment, before resuming his role as the rake. "However, she is far too bland for my palate."

"And you presume I am not?"

He grinned. "I presume there is much more to you than meets the eye, *mademoiselle*."

"Oh?"

"Oh." This time, his tone was not so blunt.

Before Penelope could demand that he leave, there was a commotion that carried from the third car to the car they were in. It was loud enough to draw everyone's attention, even the bartender's. It was a female voice, raised enough and filled with so much passion that he gave Penelope and Lucien an uncertain look. He seemed to come to the conclusion that perhaps his job as an employee of the line demanded his assistance, and he rounded the bar to exit the car. Penelope and Lucien quickly followed.

Upon opening the door to the third First Class carriage, the evidence of a heated confrontation could not be denied, even before it came into view. Cosette was arguing with the oldest concierge, who was doing his best to placate her. How it had not roused the other passengers in the car was a surprise. Yet, all the doors remained closed.

"*Adrien, I insist you do something about this,*" Cosette demanded. "*Quentin refuses to open his compartment! He could be ill, or worse!*"

She noted the arrival of Penelope, Lucien, and the

bartender and glared at them. Apparently, finding no use with the present occupants of the car, she stormed back toward the second carriage. Out of curiosity, so did Penelope, Lucien, and the bartender.

Unlike the third car, the second car was in a state over the commotion. Cosette must have caused quite the stir before seeking help in the third car. Most of the occupants in the second car had their doors opened and sported expressions of irritation, confusion, anger, and curiosity.

"*Quentin, I will not ask again. You must open Aristide's compartment!*" Cosette demanded.

Pen noted the familiar faces from dinner. Thomas and Marie occupied compartments 201 and 202, the same as Penelope and Richard in the first car. An odd arrangement for a couple on their honeymoon, especially for such a short voyage. As a married couple, they didn't need to put up the pretense of being chaste as Penelope and Richard did. Perhaps they wanted more room to themselves, and if they had the money, why not?

Compartment 205 was occupied by Mr. Gray Suit, who was still in said gray suit. Penelope frowned in confusion, as she had assumed he'd disembarked at Marseilles. Then again, the suitcase she'd seen him carrying onboard was hardly something unique. There were probably thousands of men in France alone who had such a suitcase.

The true surprise was the occupant of 203 who, just then, finally opened her door.

"*Really, this is all too much,*" Honorine said, opening her door and looking out into the corridor with droll bemusement. She was wearing a set of silk pajamas in a striking red color. She caught Cosette's eye and one side of her mouth hitched up. "*Are you really that hungry for late-night companionship?*"

"*This does not concern you,*" Cosette snapped. She turned her attention back to the poor Quentin. "*I demand that you open the door this instant!*"

"*Mademoiselle, I cannot simply open the door because Monsieur Barbier has not answered your knock. He may be asleep, and it would not be—*"

"*He is not asleep! I know what* Monsieur Barbier *sounds like when he is asleep. He could wake the dead in China with his snoring. He is not asleep and he is not answering my knock!*"

Cosette showed no sign of embarrassment at the implication that comment suggested. She was far more concerned about getting the concierge to heed her demand.

By then, the noise had alerted some of the passengers in the first car. Jules, Richard, and Lulu entered, both sporting looks of concern and curiosity.

"*If he is ill, or worse, it will be your head that I will demand. How do you think the train company will feel about allowing a man, a very important man, to die while I begged for your assistance?*"

"*Oh dear, she has threatened to have your job. I suggest you open the door, Quentin. Not to worry, I shall be sure to note you acted under duress should Monsieur Barbier also call for your head.*" Honorine seemed more amused by the spectacle than anything.

However, it did give poor Quentin a final bit of motivation. He seemed to consider both the threat and the reassurance, then sighed and pulled out his master key. Just for his own peace of mind, he knocked hard on the door to 204 one last time. "*Monsieur Barbier? Please respond if you can.*"

Cosette barely contained her impatience, still managing an eye roll. However, she kept her mouth shut as the concierge inserted the key and opened the door.

Quentin was the first to react to whatever he saw inside. "Mon Dieu!"

Cosette quickly peered inside over his shoulder...then screamed. *"He's dead!"*

CHAPTER TEN

The announcement that Monsieur Barbier was dead had everyone in the carriage rushing in to confirm it for themselves. Cosette had already pulled back, pressed against the windows of the corridor. Lucien was closest, and he managed to get a peek into compartment 204, elbowing Quentin aside to get a full view.

"*Quel désastre!*" He muttered to himself, his face contorted with distaste. Penelope thought that reaction was a bit much, considering he barely knew the man. However, murder was a shocking thing. Perhaps it was his first experience being so close to it.

Penelope wasn't new to death, and she managed a glance inside before Quentin recovered and gently moved her out of the line of sight. However, one look was all Penelope needed. Every inch of Monsieur Barbier's compartment was firmly etched into her memory, thanks to her special "photographic" ability. Even if she hadn't, the image of Monsieur Barbier slumped on the sofa with what looked like a personalized letter opener in his chest would have been difficult to erase.

"Is it true? Is he dead?" The man in 205 demanded, stepping out of his compartment.

"Oui, Monsieur Padou." Quentin said, urging him back into his own room. When Quentin turned back to face room 204, he had a grim expression, but also a slightly bewildered look in his eyes, as though he had no idea how to proceed.

"I think perhaps the conductor should be alerted. We will certainly need to alert the authorities," Richard said, his sensible presence and tone adding some calm to the situation. He eyed the bartender. "Can you do that?" The young man swallowed and nodded, then quickly went past him and the others into the first car toward the front of the train. Richard turned to Quentin. "You should close and lock the door. This is now a crime scene."

Quentin nodded quickly, his eyes darting into compartment 204 one last time, then away again. He closed the door and removed his key. "Monsieurs, Madames, please step back."

Penelope dutifully retreated several steps. Lucien was still staring at the closed door with a dark expression, only moving back when Quentin directed his gaze to him. Cosette was still frozen in place, a look of horror on her face.

"Mademoiselle Cochet, if you please?" Quentin gestured toward the third carriage, as though instructing her to return to her own accommodations.

That had Penelope feeling rather puzzled. She considered the carriage in which she was presently standing. Thomas and Marie occupied 201 and 202. Surprisingly Honorine was situated on one side of Monsieur Barbier and Monsieur Padou was on the other. Why didn't Cosette have a compartment in the same carriage as the man with whom she was seemingly traveling? She thought about following

Cosette back to her own compartment to inquire, but Richard inserted his own bit of expertise to stop that.

"I think it's wise that everyone presently in this car be gathered someplace else. As I stated, this is a crime scene and the people in these compartments may be, at the very least, witnesses to what may have happened." Richard tactfully left unstated that they were all very likely suspects as well.

"*It is the middle of the night!*" Monsieur Padou protested.

"There should be allowances for you to quickly get dressed, but I feel the conductor will agree with me on this when he arrives."

Monsieur Padou's mouth puckered with displeasure, but he retreated back into 205 and slammed the door shut, despite the fact that he was still perfectly presentable in his gray suit. Thomas and Marie, who had been oddly quiet during all of this, did the same.

"When do you suppose he was killed?" Honorine asked, looking at Quentin, then sliding her gaze to Richard, as though assessing him in his role.

"That is for the police to decide, Madame DuBois," Richard responded.

Richard's gaze finally settled on Penelope, and she could sense him studying her to see how she was handling all of this. She gave him a reassuring smile. It became slightly more sardonic when his gaze traveled to Lucien near her.

"We were in the lounge—with the bartender," she clarified, not that Richard should have needed the reassurance. "I couldn't sleep."

He nodded, but walked the length of the corridor to stand by her side. Despite the morbid circumstances, Penelope was amused to note that he made sure to stand on the side that created a buffer between Lucien and her. At the other end of the corridor, she saw that Lulu had also noted the gesture with amusement.

The bartender returned, lagging behind the conductor who rushed in with a look of shock on his face as he addressed Quentin. *"Is it true? A passenger was murdered?"*

He didn't wait for an answer, instead stalking over to the door of 204. Without waiting for the demand, Quentin quickly unlocked and opened it for him. He gasped at what it revealed. *"What happened here?"*

"I think that much is obvious, no?" Honorine answered in a droll voice.

The conductor was not amused. He turned to Quentin. *"Where were you when this happened?"*

"I...er..."

"Perhaps we should find out who was the last person to see Monsieur Barbier alive," Richard interjected, in English for Lulu's benefit. "A timeline of the evening might be in order. Everyone who had motive, means, or opportunity should be questioned, perhaps placed somewhere that isn't accessible to the scene of the crime? I suggested everyone present be secluded elsewhere. The police would surely say the same."

The conductor turned to him with a frown and a hard look. However, he also switched to English, realizing he was talking to an American. "Who might you be, Monsieur?"

"Richard Prescott, I work as a detective for the New York Police Department. I certainly don't mean to interfere or presume to tell you how to do your job. I'm sure you know how to proceed. I believe the other occupants of this car are presently getting dressed, so it wouldn't be too much of an imposition for you to have them meet in the lounge car, perhaps?"

"Yes, well…" The conductor drew his claws back in. He took a moment to think. "Yes, I think everyone in this car should be gathered in the lounge, once they are presentable."

All eyes turned to Honorine, who met them with a smile. "I have appeared in public wearing attire far more indecent than this."

"Madame…" The conductor said with a weary sigh.

"Yes, yes," she sang. She was oddly cheerful, considering the circumstances.

It did spark something in Penelope's head. She brought up the image of 204 that was still a permanent fixture in her mind. One of her suppositions had been entirely wrong, and created an even stranger picture of events taking place on board. Before she could address it, or even put it into perspective, Cosette came out of her stupor.

"There is no need to gather anyone. It's quite obvious who killed Aristide. There are only two women present with whom he argued, two women he accused of theft. This woman!" She pointed first at Honorine who had only just begun to close her door. She then swung her pointed finger in Lulu's direction. "And that one."

CHAPTER ELEVEN

On the heels of Cosette claiming that either Honorine or Lulu had killed Monsieur Barbier—first name, Aristide—there was silence. That was quickly disrupted by the ensuing uproar.

"You have no proof that Lulu killed him," Penelope protested. Lulu certainly didn't need the benefit of Pen switching to English for her sake. She had seen Cosette point the finger her way and the accusatory look in her eyes.

"Let us not forget, she was rightly cleared of any wrongdoing," Richard added.

"She most certainly was," Honorine nobly said. "As for me, I was simply a Good Samaritan, and what has that earned me? A murder accusation?" Once again, Pen noted that her reaction was rather blithe in response to the circumstances. She showed neither outrage at having been accused, nor solemnity at the fact that a murder had been committed.

"*You are no Good Samaritan,*" Cosette spat. "*I know who you really are. You are nothing but a liar and a thief, and now possibly a murderer. What are you doing on this train? What are you really after? It was Aristide, wasn't it?"*

Honorine studied her with a narrowed gaze and an enigmatic smile. It quickly cleared as she turned to address the conductor. "I think the suggestion that we all gather is a fine one. This, naturally, would include those closest to Monsieur Barbier. I shall get dressed at once."

Before anyone could respond, she had retreated back into her room and closed the door. Penelope was still focused on what Cosette had just said about her. She wasn't the only one.

"What did you mean, just now?" The conductor asked. *"Do you know this woman? Do you have proof she had an ulterior motive?"*

Cosette blinked and turned her attention to him. "I, er..." She inhaled and sported a haughtier expression. *"She stole Aristide's wallet earlier. She will claim to have found it and returned it, but anyone could see that was a lie."*

"Was anything stolen?"

"I am not sure. The only one who does know is Aristide, who is inconveniently dead."

"I should point out," Penelope said, using English in the hopes that the two of them would as well for Lulu's benefit, "Monsieur Barbier checked his wallet and confirmed in front of several witnesses that nothing was stolen."

"But what was she doing with it in the first place?" Cosette demanded, reluctantly switching to English as well.

"How do you know her?" Penelope asked, getting back to the more important question the conductor had asked.

Cosette stared at her with a cool look. "I don't. It was nothing more than an...expression, is that how you say it?"

Penelope couldn't have been the only one who could quite clearly see she was lying. Did she know Honorine? If so, how? Madame DuBois was certainly an interesting and enigmatic character. Why had she taken Monsieur Barbier's wallet, if not for his money?

"*Alors*, I must insist that everyone please proceed to the lounge area in the dining car. Madames, Monsieurs, if you will?" The conductor made a point of looking at Penelope, Richard, Lucien, Cosette, and Lulu. "Are your quarters in another carriage?"

"I am in the third car," Lucien responded, then eyed Cosette with a teasingly suggestive look. "As is Mademoiselle Cochet."

Cosette sniffed, glared at him, then without another word pushed past everyone to head to the fourth carriage where the lounge was.

"*Mica, if you will, please return to your station. Please keep watch over everyone who enters, and* please *make sure no one drinks.*" the conductor said to the bartender, who nodded and quickly followed Cosette.

"Miss Banks, Miss Simmons, and I are in the first carriage," Richard said to him.

The conductor nodded and sighed, then turned to Jules. "*I'm afraid you will have to rouse everyone else in that car. Have them get dressed and join us in the lounge. I think it best that all passengers and employees in First Class are there together for their safety.*" He turned to Quentin. "*Please tell Adrien in the third carriage to have any remaining passengers there join us as well.*"

"*It is only Monsieur Vollant and Mademoiselle Cochet occupying rooms in the third carriage, I am afraid,*" Quentin answered.

"*Is that so?*" The conductor seemed surprised by that. "*Ah well, collect Adrien all the same. He can help you maintain order.*"

Penelope was also surprised by that news. She knitted her brows, wondering if that arrangement was by design. Not only was Cosette not traveling in the same car as Aristide Barbier, but she and Lucien were alone together in the third car. The tickets for First Class were not trivial in terms of cost, but it still seemed odd to have three entire sleeper compartments remain empty, even in the summer when only Americans traveled to the French Riviera on holiday.

The conductor continued. "Quentin, I would like to speak with you alone when you return." His tone was censuring, and the poor conductor understandably sported a worried expression.

Richard and Lulu returned to the second car to change into something more appropriate than a robe over their nightclothes. Penelope reentered the lounge car with Lucien. Cosette was already there, sitting in one of the armchairs, one elegant leg crossed over the other. She gave the two arrivals a look that indicated she was not interested in company.

Penelope had never allowed such niceties to preclude satisfying her curiosity, especially in the face of murder. "You have my condolences, Mademoiselle Cochet. Were you and Monsieur Barbier particularly close?"

Lucien snorted in amusement.

Cosette glared at her, then dismissively turned to look out the window without answering.

"It's just that, I would have thought, the third car being so empty, he might have bought tickets for compartments closer together."

Cosette's attention remained focused on the window, but Penelope could see her jaw clenched with irritation or anger.

Lucien laughed. "*Oh, come now, Cosette, are you so shy all of a sudden? It is no secret what your, ah, relationship with Monsieur Barbier is—or should I say, was? Though yes, one does wonder about the sleeping arrangements. I would have thought he would have been more accommodating in that regard. It is shameful. To have you entering an entirely separate car just to—*"

"*Shut up!*" Cosette spat, finally turning around. Penelope had the distinct idea he had been goading her to do just that. "*You know nothing of my relationship with him, and I would ask that you keep such inappropriate suggestions to yourself.*"

"*Very fortunate, you encountering Monsieur Barbier—or was it Aristide?—on holiday in the Côte d'Azur. It is a shame about the murder. If I had known the third car would be so empty, I would have made good use of my access to compartment 304 before now.*"

Cosette met him with an icy look of derision. "*My door would have remained firmly closed and locked. Speaking of fortunate encounters, what was your business in the south of France?*"

"*Beautiful women with their legs on display,*" Lucien said with a wink.

Cosette exhaled with exasperation, as though she regretted taking his bait. She quickly turned to stare out the window again, tugging her skirt further down past her knees. By then, Adrien had entered. He looked understandably stunned by the news of the murder, and rushed over to chat with Mica behind the bar.

Penelope was still considering a few things Lucien had said that certainly needed clarification. "So Cosette and you are the *only* occupants of the third car?"

"Yes, we are," he said, turning his lecherous attention

her way, as though that was an invitation to something more.

Penelope ignored it, still set on getting answers. There were only three First Class carriages on the train. "So, the two gentlemen I sat with at dinner aren't staying in your carriage?"

"No?" He seemed to consider that, now that she had mentioned it. Even Cosette turned her head slightly, as though she was suddenly paying more attention. Penelope didn't have to voice the question that was on all their minds: Which car were Simon and André staying in?

CHAPTER TWELVE

"Adrien!" Lucien called out, drawing the attention of the concierge for the third car. He and Mica were still huddled together in intense conversation. There was no doubt as to the topic they were discussing, as evidenced by the ashen look of shock that was still on both faces when they turned to acknowledge Lucien.

"Yes, Monsieur Vollant," Adrien said, instantly approaching with the professionalism that had been instilled in him. "How may I be of service?"

"Do you know all the passengers on board the train, or at least those in First Class?" Penelope asked him.

His brow lifted ever so slightly at the question. "Oui, the concierges are given information on all passengers in the First Class carriages."

It was a diplomatic response, not giving away too much information. However, Lucien was anything but a diplomatic man. "Yes, yes, but what about the other cars? For instance, the two gentlemen who joined us at dinner, which to my understanding is reserved for First Class passengers?"

He turned to Penelope, encouraging her to provide more context.

"Simon Pougnet and André Robineau were their names, and yes, they sat next to Mr. Prescott and me at dinner. However, it seems they don't have First Class accommodations?"

Adrien hid any reaction quite well, maintaining his steady composure and neutral expression at the mention of their names. However, Penelope noted a flicker of familiarity in his eyes. "I will certainly look into this for you, mademoiselle."

He knew, but for some reason he was not at liberty to mention anything more about them.

Lucien was indignant. "I hope you know I paid quite a bit of money for this ticket. If they are just allowing anyone to indulge in the same benefits afforded to me, then what is the point?"

"Again, I will certainly look into this, Monsieur Vollant."

Lucien muttered under his breath in French and walked past him to the bar. "*I don't care what that conductor says, I would like a drink.*" At the protest from the bartender he waved a hand in the air. "*If I'm to be penned here like a dog, I demand a drink. Pour me a finger of cognac or I will grab the bottle myself.*"

The poor bartender, Mica, gave a helpless look to Adrien, who ever so subtly nodded. Penelope supposed it was better to have a passenger mollified with a drop of brandy than to have a belligerent one making a scene. Hopefully, it might even help lubricate his mouth so he would provide more information about certain things. She still had a number of questions she wanted satisfied.

"Did you and Marie meet on this train?" Penelope

asked once Lucien had his brandy, wisely not quite a full finger.

"Marie?"

"The woman with whom you were conversing when I entered this car earlier."

"Ah, is that her name?" He put on a good show of feigning ignorance. "We were just discussing...the treasures of France."

"It seemed rather heated."

He met her with a sly look. "I do tend to elicit such passion in women."

Penelope refrained from rolling her eyes. "Odd for a woman to be so, ah, *passionate* about another man while coming back from her own honeymoon."

"Yes...honeymoon," Lucien purred, some secret bit of cynicism in his tone. He chuckled before adding, "Perhaps she was left disappointed?"

"Or perhaps it wasn't the treasures of France you were discussing?"

He finally turned to her with a frank look. "What is it you are asking, mademoiselle?"

What was it she was asking? She wanted an honest answer to everything he seemed to be disguising underneath his suggestive remarks and leery looks. It was enough to leave most women keeping a firm distance—and perhaps not asking too many pointed questions—but Penelope was made of sterner stuff.

Before she could ask another question, the other passengers began trickling in. The first to arrive were Marie and Thomas. The former, immediately glanced Lucien's way, then quickly averted her eyes, which were filled with trepidation. Next to her, Thomas was already glaring at him, communicating some message that had Lucien chuckling softly. They settled in on the opposite side of the bar area, as far away from Lucien as possible.

That only had Penelope even more curious. Had Marie done something as daft as tell her husband about her interaction with Lucien? Penelope didn't think so. Only a woman looking to make a man jealous, and possibly incite a potentially violent confrontation, would do such a thing. Marie may have been meek, but she didn't appear to be stupid or reckless. The question as to what they had been arguing about would have to remain a mystery for now.

Monsieur Padou then entered, which sparked a note in Penelope's mind. However, Richard entered soon after him, temporarily taking her mind away from that thought. He noted her proximity to Lucien and his step quickened as he approached. His eyes remained trained on the man as he closed the distance and put a possessive arm around her. Penelope smiled at the unnecessary gesture, even as he not-so-subtly walked her a few feet away from Lucien.

"I hope Cousin Cordelia wasn't too terribly upset at the news."

"That's what caused the delay in coming here. I had to temper Benny's excitement at the news, and console your cousin enough that she could get dressed and come here. She was still changing as I left."

"Perhaps a bit of brandy might do her some good," Pen said, eyeing the glass in Lucien's hand.

Lucien had once again set his sights on Cosette. Penelope was beginning to feel sorry for the young woman again, despite the earlier accusation she had made of Lulu. She was surprised to see that Cosette didn't instantly dismiss him with a curt remark. Instead, she leaned in, a serious look on her face, seemingly asking him a question. Lucien gave a short answer, then leaned back in his chair. Penelope couldn't see his facial expression but his body seemed relaxed. Cosette remained in place, her face strained with irritation and impatience as he idly sipped his brandy. Now, he was the one pointedly ignoring her.

It really was odd how people who were seemingly strangers on this train were interacting with one another. It was only natural that some people, those with more sociable tendencies, might make fast friends during a voyage, even as one as short as the current one. However, it seemed more and more as though they were all playing a game, taunting and teasing each other, like rival players in a sport, though much more subtly.

The only one who didn't seem to be playing was Monsieur Padou. Penelope transferred her attention to him, where he sat at a table by himself reading a large book, still an isolated stranger to everyone else.

"That's it!" Penelope whispered as the thing that had been nagging her finally fell into place.

"What is it?" Richard asked.

"Cousin Cordelia is in cabin 105."

"Yes."

"I assume you saw the inside of it while you were consoling her?"

"Yes, though I wasn't paying that much attention to the compartment at the time. It didn't seem any different from yours or mine."

"No, it didn't. And Benny's, you glimpsed inside his as well?

"Yes, briefly. What is this all about, Penelope?"

"There is no door to room 103 in your compartment."

"Lucille's room?" He quirked an eyebrow, then sported a bemused smile. "No, my dear, there isn't."

"And Benny doesn't have a door to compartment 103 either?"

Richard wrinkled his brow in thought, then shook his head. "I don't think it does. Why?"

"Because I was wrong about which compartments are connected. I assumed 103 and 104 were connected, but they aren't. However, compartments ending in 4 *do* have a door that leads to those that end in 5, and vice versa. Lucien inadvertently confirmed that was the case in the third carriage—304 connects to 305." She turned to study Lucien and Cosette, who were back to pretending the other didn't exist.

"Why is that important?" Richard asked, following Penelope's gaze as it landed on Monsieur Padou. That was enough for him to answer his own question. "Because he is in compartment 205."

"Which has a door leading directly to where Aristide Barbier's body was found in 204," Penelope said.

CHAPTER THIRTEEN

If Monsieur Padou noticed Penelope's and Richard's attention on him, he studiously ignored it. However, others in the room noted it. Marie and Thomas had glanced their way and followed their gaze to the man who sat at a table, lazily perusing the pages of the large book he had brought with him to the lounge.

Before Richard could stop her, Penelope ambled over. Fortunately, he didn't follow. He probably realized that two people approaching Monsieur Padou would do nothing but intimidate him, especially when one of them had already announced himself as a detective. They had both also seen the way he reacted to Cosette as they passed one another at dinner. Some men were easily disarmed, or at least distracted by pretty women. Penelope was not Mademoiselle Cochet, but she had turned her fair share of heads.

Before she reached him, Penelope noted the slight whiff of something acrid radiating from his vicinity. Perhaps Monsieur Padou had dabbed on a bit of cologne before retiring to the lounge. He was almost certainly unattached, as any woman would have told him how awful it was. There was a familiar tinge to it. It made Penelope think of the pungent, eye-watering odors of a carpentry shop or an artist's studio, though this wasn't quite that strong.

When she was close enough, Penelope idly glanced at the pages of the book. It was at least twice the size of a regular book, with pristine binding and pages filled mostly with illustrations of the human skeleton. The thick pages were frayed enough to denote constant perusal.

"Fascinating, isn't it?" Monsieur Padou said, not bothering to look up from the book. "Yes, Gray's is the Bible, so to speak, when it comes to human anatomy for the medical community, but I prefer Cunningham's. It's much more rare, of course, difficult to find an original, though I confess this is a reprinting. Cunningham looks at the human body with the eye of an artist not a medical professional. Note the pose of this arm and hand here, presenting the ensemble as it would naturally function on the human subject, arm hooked, fingers curved, as though gesturing toward something. The conductor was kind enough to let me take it with me. I suspect we may be isolated here in the lounge for quite some time. Particularly those of us in the second carriage." He finally turned to acknowledge her with a blithe smile. "How can I help you, Mademoiselle Banks?"

He had an accent that was not quite French. There were hints of German in the way he pronounced certain words. Swiss, was what Penelope first assumed, or perhaps he came from a region of France that was closer to the eastern border.

"Monsieur Barbier was last seen at dinner, a dinner in which many people excused themselves, including you?"

She had posed it as a question to elicit a response. Any response would do. The man was still very much a mystery.

"Yes."

Penelope realized she would have to be more direct. "Did you know Monsieur Barbier at all?"

"How could I have possibly known him?" He didn't seem surprised, upset, or even suspicious of the question.

"Your compartment, it shares a door with his."

"A coincidence. Mine has been firmly locked this entire trip. I assume his was as well."

"It was certainly an insult to Mademoiselle Cochet, as he seemed to have been *her* traveling companion," Pen said, casting a glance her way. Cosette was carefully observing them over Lucien's shoulder.

Monsieur Padou's quiet laugh brought her attention back. He was also staring at Cosette, then turned his attention back to Penelope. "I doubt she is very much put out by the arrangement. However, to answer your *unasked* question, I did not kill Monsieur Barbier. I did not know the man, thus, I have no motive."

There was no way for Penelope to prove otherwise. The two men had not so much as glanced at one another during the entire voyage, at least that she saw. Even Cosette's gaze was one of curiosity, not familiarity. She didn't seem to know Monsieur Padou either. It was time to try another avenue of questioning.

"Are you a doctor?" Pen asked, innocuous curiosity in her voice.

His smile was dry, as though he was fully aware that she was fishing for information. "I am not."

She smiled in a slightly vapid way to charm him. "Just a bibliophile I suppose?"

His smile thinned and he closed his book, placing a possessive hand on the cover, as though the answer were obvious. "I am."

There was a dismissive tone in his voice, which was

punctuated by the way his beady eyes bored into Penelope as though shooing her away with nothing more than his gaze. Having no further avenues of conversation that might lead to a clue, she offered a final smile and left. He was by then far too suspicious to reveal anything of value.

"Did you learn anything?"

"He likes books and has awful taste in cologne."

"He *must* like books to bring such a tome with him on vacation."

Penelope turned to look at it again. Monsieur Padou had given up looking at the artistic representations of the human skeletal structure in favor of the darkness outside the window. Unlike the frayed pages of the book, the cover was practically brand new. He must have had it recently rebound. It was an odd thing to bring to the Riviera, or Paris, depending on which was his original destination. Perhaps he was headed to Lyon? He seemed to have only the one brown suitcase with him, so it may have been a working trip. Particularly, if he hadn't bothered packing a change of clothes or something to sleep in. The thought made her briefly wonder whose brown suitcase had been taken off the train in Marseilles.

Penelope's attention, along with everyone else's in the bar area, was snagged by the moaning wails of the one First Class passenger with the most delicate of nerves. Cousin Cordelia was escorted in by Benny and Lulu, each on one side of her. Jules was right behind them.

"I just don't understand how something like this could happen—and on a train? I was led to believe this was a fine company with a respectable reputation. Who would do such a thing?"

"There, there, dove, you're perfectly safe in here." Benny cooed, patting the arm hooked through his. "It was no doubt a crime of passion." He shot Penelope a droll look, as though to suggest the most tawdry motive for the murder.

"Let's sit down," Lulu said, leading her to the small couch.

"Oh look, they're allowing us to drink after all. Thank goodness for that," Benny said, eyeing Lucien's hand holding a drink. "Shall I get you a drop of medicine, dove?"

Cousin Cordelia nodded, no doubt eager for her usual finger of brandy.

"Monsieur, I'm afraid the instructions were quite clear. We are not allowed—"

"I will have one as well," Cosette interrupted, shooting up from her chair and strutting to the bar along with Benny.

"There now, a true democracy at work," he said approvingly.

"But—" Mica gave a pleading look to Jules. Adrien had conveniently gone to use the facilities.

Jules cleared his throat, taking charge. "I think, perhaps just one might be safe. We don't want a, how do you say, revolution?"

"Revolt? Mutiny? Riot? Catastrophe? Unraveling at the seams?"

"I think he sees your point, Benjamin," Richard said. "And I think a small drink, just enough to settle anyone's nerves, will be fine. It will be a while before we reach our next stop in Lyon."

Jules nodded in agreement and gave Mica a pointed look. "Very small."

Penelope refrained, her thoughts focused on the image in her head of the murder scene. Aristide's bed hadn't been turned down, but otherwise it would have been difficult to tell the difference between his room and hers. Of course, her room didn't have a man whose chest had been impaled with a letter opener engraved with the initials A.B. on it. Also, Penelope at least had a small suitcase, a change of clothes, and a book. Monsieur Barbier only had his untouched dinner, still on the tray that Quentin had brought to him. Like Monsieur Padou, he'd still been in his suit, though with his stained jacket still removed. There was no luggage visible in the picture in her head, but that wasn't odd. It may have been in the small closet next to the bed, as hers was.

One thing she now noted was that the lock on the doors between compartments in the image in her memory was turned vertically: locked. Penelope should know, as it had been decidedly horizontal for her rendezvous with Richard only a few hours ago. No doubt Monsieur Padou's door in 205 was also locked, which negated the idea that he had used that door to gain ingress into Monsieur Barbier's room. How could he have locked the door in 204 from his own compartment? In fact, Monsieur Barbier's room had been locked to the corridor as well, as Quentin had needed to use his key to unlock it. So how had the killer escaped?

CHAPTER FOURTEEN

"I know that look," Richard said next to Penelope. "What have you just discovered?"

"Monsieur Barbier's room was locked from the inside."

"Yes, that much was established from the ruckus created by Mademoiselle Cochet. She was the one to insist that the concierge open the door."

"I can also tell you that the door leading to compartment 205 was locked. So how did the killer escape?"

"Obviously they took the key with them."

"They must have," Penelope said thoughtfully. "And I doubt they still have that key on them. Right now, it's probably lying in some field along the tracks miles away."

"That, of course, still leaves almost everyone as a suspect, depending on when Monsieur Barbier was last seen alive."

"We last saw him at dinner, when he spilled his soup, blaming Cosette of course, and excused himself. He then decided to finish dinner in his compartment."

"At least according to her."

"Yes. Convenient that *she* would insist he didn't want to

be disturbed and instructed his meal be left outside his door."

"That's also a bit obvious, isn't it? If she is the killer, she practically announced it in front of everyone. And then to come back and insist his room be opened in the middle of the night?"

"You're awfully quick to defend her," Penelope said, arching an eyebrow.

"I just have a sense that she's smarter than she appears—more cunning, if you will."

Penelope followed his glance toward Cosette. Richard had a point. Penelope had known many a woman who sought out a rich man to provide for them. Most of them were indeed smarter than anyone gave them credit for—more cunning, at any rate. Pen couldn't fault them. It was easy enough to be born into money, and her most recent fortune had been bequeathed to her by a family friend. That gave her a lot of independence that women like Cosette weren't afforded. She must have been quite the charming *fille* to have caught Aristide's eye in Menton, or wherever it was that they boarded. It was pointless trying to cozy up to her for a bit of questioning. If Monsieur Padou was quick to uncover Penelope's aims, Cosette would be even quicker.

It also suddenly occurred to Penelope that she'd seen the tray of food inside Monsieur Barbier's compartment when they had found his body. How had it gotten there if he'd been dead when Cosette returned to the dining room?

"There were several people who left during dinner," Richard said. "Monsieur Padou was first, but he returned before Cosette even had a chance to reach Aristide's door. When Quentin arrived to see to his dinner tray, Thomas left, then Marie. Quite interesting timing, don't you think?"

They both turned their attention to Marie and Thomas, who sat a little too stiffly, as though each of them was ready to spring up and bolt at the drop of a hat. They were definitely worried about something, but did that spell murder?

"Honorine, and then Lucien left, but that was after Quentin had returned to the first sleeper car to deliver Aristide's dinner," Richard continued.

"It's easy enough to distract even an attentive concierge. Something tells me those two are tricksters. Lucien is the fox and Honorine is...well, I can't quite grasp what she is. If she is a murderer, she is quite a charming one."

"Speaking of which, where *is* the oh-so-charming Madame DuBois?" Richard glanced toward the entrance to the car, as though expecting her to enter at any moment.

"She must be inserting herself into the investigation. Or perhaps they are questioning her about the wallet theft?"

"So you still think she stole it?" Richard offered a wry smile.

"Don't you?"

He laughed softly and nodded. "The question is, why?"

It was then that Madame Honorine DuBois breezed in, a placid smile on her face as though she hadn't a care in the world, or as though a murder hadn't just been committed in the room next to hers. Her dark eyes instantly swiveled to Penelope and a gleam came to them as she approached.

"Mademoiselle Banks, is it?"

"Yes. Please call me Penelope." Pen figured it would be worthwhile ingratiating herself to draw more information.

"Penelope, of course. But the name Banks...." Honorine scrutinized her. "Tell me, did your mother happen to visit the 1900 Paris Exhibition as well?"

Penelope blinked in surprise. "Yes, not too long after my

father and she were married. It was during their honeymoon."

"And...do you have any siblings?"

"No, it's just me." Penelope wondered what was the point of this line of discussion. Was it simply a distraction?

"Ah." Honorine laughed in a tinkling sort of way, earning her a few looks of disapproval. Penelope would have been one of them if she hadn't still been lost in confusion. All the more so when Honorine leaned in with a conspiratorial smile. "I believe you were there as well?"

Penelope was shocked even more, this time into a coughing fit. Richard patted her lightly on the back, frowning at the cause of it. Honorine laughed lightly again. The news wasn't a surprise to Penelope. Her mother had hinted at just such a thing often enough for Penelope to understand once she was old enough. However, she couldn't imagine Juliette Banks would have advertised such a delicate condition to a stranger, even if she was never one to have her corset strings too tightly bound. While that sort of talk was slightly less taboo in the modern age, it certainly hadn't been back then.

"She told you that?"

"Oh no, I have enough nieces and nephews to tell." She tilted her head and offered a cryptic smile to Penelope, allowing it to linger a moment before she continued. "She looks so much like you, except for the eyes—green not blue."

"Yes," Penelope said, feeling herself get emotional at the loss. Her mother had died during the Great Influenza when Pen was only nineteen.

"She is no longer with us?" Honore said in a sympathetic tone.

"No, she isn't."

"*Quelle tragédie.* It is always the brightest stars that

blink away too quickly. She was the one who suggested I try the corn pancakes. I met her when her jade hair comb fell out and I rescued it for her."

Penelope narrowed her eyes, wondering if her mother's jade comb—a treasured and sentimental piece that had been gifted to Penelope—had been "rescued" or stolen. "Did you?"

Honorine must have sensed the accusation in her tone. Rather than be offended, she was amused, laughing softly again. "I am not a thief, Mademoiselle Banks. At least not when it comes to the innocent."

Penelope's brow wrinkled in confusion. Before she could ask what that meant, Honorine had breezed away.

"Ah, I see we have been allowed drinks, after all. *Quelle merveille*, I shall take champagne!"

"Did that sound like a confession to you?" Penelope muttered to Richard.

"It did. I think it's safe to say she really did steal Monsieur Barbier's wallet."

"What do you suppose she thinks he's guilty of?"

"Whatever it is, it may very well be the thing that got him killed."

CHAPTER FIFTEEN

The conductor entered the dining and bar car. Trailing behind him was Quentin, looking as though he had just received an earful regarding his duties, or lack thereof. In his defense, being on the lookout for murder was hardly a standard job requirement for a train concierge.

If there was one person who could properly identify the windows of opportunity for murder since Monsieur Barbier had last been seen it was Quentin. As concierge for the second sleeper car, he would be able to say who had entered and left the car, and when. Surely no one would have been bold enough to commit murder while he was present.

"*Mica, have you poured drinks? I gave strict instructions!*" The conductor gave the poor bartender a withering look, then offered the same to the senior concierge.

"*It was my doing,*" Jules said, bravely stepping forward. "*Adrien and Mica are not to blame.*"

"*So* you *are in charge now?*" The conductor transferred his wrath to Jules.

"In his defense, there threatened to be a minor mutiny. I think, considering the circumstances, a small drink to settle everyone's nerves is not out of the question," Richard interjected. "We do have several hours before we reach our next stop in Lyon. I doubt anyone will still be too inebriated by then to be interviewed by the police."

The conductor studied him, not pleased, but also not quite as irate as he was before. He nodded. "Oui, well..." He rubbed his chin, as though considering how to proceed.

"Have Monsieur Pougnet and Monsieur Robineau departed the train? Perhaps in Marseilles?" Penelope asked.

The conductor blinked, his attention snapping to her. "They are of no concern."

"I think they are very much a concern, especially if they are still on board. They left dinner before dessert was served. It seems they aren't residing in any of the First Class sleeper carriages, so where are they? They left in that direction after dinner, which means they may have gone through the second sleeper car, right past Monsieur Barbier's room. Unless they are in Marseille, they should be in this lounge with us."

"Perhaps it would be wise to bring them in to join us," Richard said, quickly adding, "even if they are not presently in a First Class sleeper car."

The conductor stared at him, his mouth set with reluctance, before he sighed and nodded to Adrien. The third car concierge quietly departed to fetch them. Pen noted, that rather than go in the direction of the sleeper cars toward the front of the train, he headed through the dining room and the kitchen beyond. So, the two men were in second class? Perhaps their attendance at dinner, and earlier in the lounge, would be explained when they were brought back.

The conductor turned back to face the passengers. *"Does everyone speak French?"*

"We have one in our group who doesn't, Monsieur," Penelope said, nodding to Lulu.

"We would prefer English as well," Thomas said.

The conductor was diplomatic about it, but Pen noted that inevitable hint of French disdain for anyone who didn't speak the language. "Would English be acceptable to everyone else?" When there was no protest, he continued. "Very well, I shall use English. I do apologize for the disruption. However, it appears a murder has been committed in the second of our First Class sleeper cars. Thus, it remains a crime scene."

"Must we all be kept from our rooms? I and Mademoiselle Cochet are in the third car," Lucien protested.

"For now, yes, I am afraid. We may be able to allow you back to your rooms once I get more information from the authorities or my superiors. This is as much for your safety as it is for protecting the integrity of the scene. To put it quite bluntly, one or more of the individuals in this room is a murderer."

Although that much was understood, having him put it so frankly sent a ripple of unease through the room. There were a few murmurs and a brief whimper from Cousin Cordelia.

"It seems one or more of you were accused of stealing Monsieur Barbier's wallet?" The conductor looked around the room.

Cosette suddenly seemed to regret having made the earlier accusation. "I was upset at the time. I did not mean to imply either woman was guilty of murder."

"All the same, I would like to know more. Was a wallet stolen or not? If Monsieur Barbier made an accusation against anyone, that may be important. Certainly that speaks to motive?"

"It was *found*, not stolen," Honorine answered, then added with a smile, "By me. And yes, there was an accusation made by Monsieur Barbier. However, it was quickly resolved when it was understood nothing had been stolen."

"Is that really true?" Penelope dared to ask. "Not everything that can be stolen is in physical form. Perhaps it was information you were after?"

That accusation seemed to trigger a note of alarm in everyone—everyone save for Honorine.

Cosette breathed out a soft, humorless laugh and gave Honorine a sardonic look. "That frivolous story about visiting Monte Carlo. Ha! Did you at least find what it was you were after in his wallet? Anyone could have seen you were after something from Aristide. And to so conveniently have a room next to his? What was it you were really after? Did you kill him?"

"It does paint a rather interesting picture," Lucien mused, turning around to assess Honorine through narrowed eyes.

"I would like to know as well. What is it you were after, Madame?" Thomas demanded.

"Did you find *anything*?" Marie asked in a surprisingly pleading tone, earning her a censuring look from her husband.

Penelope realized Monsieur Padou had never reopened his book. He now stared at Honorine with a piercing look, as though he could get the answers out of her if he simply studied her hard enough.

But it was Honorine who was the most surprising. She took every barb thrown at her with leather skin. Each fell away under the unconcerned smile she sported.

"You are correct, Mademoiselle Banks, it was information I was after."

Before she could continue Adrien returned with Simon and André. They were still in their suits, either because they had no intention of sleeping or they hadn't been afforded sleeper compartments. They looked around with an air of authority, and suddenly Penelope had an inkling as to their role on board the train.

"Ah, you are just in time, I was just about to explain who I really am," Honorine said, as though she too knew who they really were.

Simon Pougnet stared at her with a look that indicated he knew from the very start she would be nothing but trouble. "There is no need to explain who you are, Madame DuBois. Anyone who works with criminals is well aware of your reputation."

CHAPTER SIXTEEN

Simon's declaration about Honorine had everyone oddly silent. Was Honorine a criminal? She had indicated that once upon a time she had been accused of murder.

Penelope should not have been surprised at Honorine's inability to become dispossessed of her composure. Still, even in the face of such an accusation, she remained serene and, as always, mildly amused.

"Perhaps it is not I who should be explaining myself," Honorine said, studying Simon. "Who are you two gentlemen? And please do not bore us with the mundane story about visiting a friend in Menton."

Simon and André stared at one another, some unspoken understanding passing between them before the former addressed everyone. "We are with the International Criminal Police Commission, here on official business."

"International?" Thomas said, his face contorted with concern. "What does an international agency have to do with this murder?"

"Our business here is none of your concern," André

snapped, giving him a look meant to silence all further inquiry.

"It's quite obvious that Monsieur Barbier was their concern," Honorine answered, giving both men an assessing look. For once, she didn't seem impassive or blasé. In fact, she seemed confused.

"But it seems Monsieur Barbier has been murdered," Simon said, studying her just as hard. "So perhaps you might tell us what information you were after, Madame DuBois? And please do not bore us with the mundane story that you simply found his wallet."

Honorine was pensive at first, as though wondering whether she should say anything or not. It lasted only a brief moment, long enough for one to notice, but not so long that she had serious reservation about answering truthfully.

"I represent Monsieur Barbier's wife, his *estranged* wife. As you seem to already know, I am a private investigator."

All eyes instantly went to Cosette, who simply looked back with an insolent, cool gaze, as though she thought it silly for them to suddenly start judging her in her presumed role. However, Penelope wondered if she was the only one to notice Marie's sharp intake of breath, and the way Thomas instantly grabbed her wrist, as though to silence her.

"And what is this mission his wife has sent you on?" André inquired, even more intrigued.

"He has a substantial portion of her fortune and has been hiding it from her. I was hired to find it. That is all." Honorine gave both men a keen look. "Though, I find it odd that the International Police would be interested in such a common bit of deceit. Even my own husband, may he rest in peace, was not honest when it came to finances."

So, Aristide Barbier was a despicable reprobate. That

wasn't a surprise to Penelope. Nor was it a surprise to find out Honorine wasn't such a bad sort—if she was telling the truth. Pen liked to think she was at least a decent judge of character, and she had honestly liked Honorine, even if she had been suspicious of her motives. As it turned out, they had a lot in common, both of them private investigators. Considering her age, Penelope wondered how long Honorine had been working as such.

However, there were others in the cabin she was far more interested in at the moment. Marie still stared at Honorine like a puppy eager to jump on her, in her case for information. Thomas's hand on her wrist seemed to be the only thing holding her back. Why would a newlywed British couple be interested in the financial battles of an older French couple? Did they know Madame Barbier, or perhaps her recently deceased husband? Did that mean they had motive?

"I am curious," Lucien said, his gaze settled on Cosette with a taunting glint. "Just how much does Madame Barbier claim her husband is hiding?"

"Two million francs."

Lucien coughed out a laugh, which only shined a light on his lack of scruples. He seemed even more amused when Cosette's mouth fell open in indignation. She noted everyone's attention was still directed her way and quickly caught herself, replacing it with placid indifference. It seemed hiding money from his wife did nothing to trouble her scruples, but hiding money from his mistress was a step too far. But did that translate to murder?

Something about Cosette's reaction created a loose thread in Penelope's brain that she felt like picking at to see if it unraveled a clue to her guilt for murder. It was the reaction to the two million francs, most notably her indignation.

Then, there was Lucien. Why had he asked the question about money, particularly while giving Cosette such a taunting look? It was natural for someone who wanted to tease her to poke at the most sensitive spot. After all, her relationship with the deceased was, by all appearances, strictly financial. However, there appeared to be more to it than that. They had the entire third car to themselves, oddly enough—a thought that pulled at another string in Penelope's mind. At that rate, she'd have nothing but a head filled with stray threads, each nagging her for attention. Pen shook it, hoping to clear away some of the distraction to focus on what was happening at the moment.

Simon and André were still focused on Honorine, not quite done with their interrogation. "What else did you discover in your investigation?"

"Not very much, I only just encountered him here on the train. My information was incorrect, as I had been told he would be boarding the train in Monte Carlo. However, it seems he was in fact in Menton." She twisted her mouth with mild irritation before adding, "Still, I was lucky to get a First Class ticket, the last one, it seems."

"The last one?" Penelope blurted out in surprise.

"Yes, it was quite fortuitous," Honorine said happily.

Penelope's eyes darted to Lucien and Cosette. They both seemed put out, but not surprised. So, Penelope was the one to directly address it.

"That makes no sense. The third class car is empty, save for these two." She gestured to Lucien and Cosette, the latter of whom was still not making eye contact with anyone in the room. "And, no offense Mademoiselle Cochet, but why would he have purchased tickets for the two of you so far away from one another?"

That earned a soft chuckle from Lucien, which earned him an icy glare from Cosette.

"They are involved with one another, that is why. She has been consorting with Lucien all while traveling with Monsieur Barbier," Thomas spat. "He must have sussed out what they were up to. One or both of them has killed him for it."

Cosette coughed out an incredulous laugh. Lucien twisted around in his seat to offer a look of overt amusement at the accusation.

"*Moi*? With *him*?" Cosette exclaimed. "I would never. My tastes are far more sophisticated than that. This one, you can find scouring the gutters for his fare."

A wicked grin laced Lucien's mouth. "The gutter can be ripe with surprisingly charming fare." He turned to give Cosette a sardonic smile. "However, I think you'll find status does not translate to sophistication." Cosette rolled her eyes to the side with indifference. Lucien snapped his attention back to Thomas with a renewed grin. "But alas, you are very incorrect, mon ami, I could never hope to afford the services of Mademoiselle *Cochet*. Though, she does have quite the reputation. She'll do anything for a price." He waggled his eyes suggestively.

That final comment was what tugged loose one of the threads in Penelope's head. She finally realized what was nagging her about Cosette.

"Now, I see it," she muttered. It was loud enough to have several heads turned her way. Hers was directed toward Cosette. "She isn't at all who she appears to be."

CHAPTER SEVENTEEN

All eyes were on Penelope, now that she had announced she had discovered something about Cosette, though she had yet to reveal what it was. The accused woman simply stared back, her face a mask of neutrality, but Pen could see the burning in her eyes, either from alarm, anger, or curiosity. It only confirmed that she had been right about the woman not being what she seemed.

"To be fair, you haven't exactly stated what your relationship to Monsieur Barbier was," Penelope began. "However, you haven't dispelled the notion that you are a kept woman, or perhaps something even more casual. After all, Monsieur Barbier was neither attractive nor charming enough to be with purely for romantic reasons."

That got a slight rise of indignation out of Cosette, but she remained quiet and watchful.

"Penelope, that's a horrid accusation," Cousin Cordelia scolded. She *would* be the only one innocent enough to think the best of people.

"But quite accurate...in a manner of speaking," Lucien said in a suggestive tone.

"And you?" Cosette spat. "What kind of man are you, if you can even be called one? I think perhaps a weasel is more likely. What are *you* doing on this train?"

"Ah, but we are discussing you, ma cherie," he said with a laugh, then turned to Penelope. "*S'il vous plaît*, continue mademoiselle."

Penelope had become distracted by Cosette's outburst. She and Lucien were obviously much closer than Pen had assumed. That made them having an entire car to themselves, strange enough as that was, even more interesting. However, everyone was waiting for her to expound on her accusation of Cosette, including the accused herself.

"There were subtle things, for example, your dress. It's expensive, modern, an Edward Molyneux, no? Certainly not inexpensive. But it's from the Spring line, which would have come out sometime in February, nearly six months ago. It wasn't purchased by Monsieur Barbier, though was it? A woman like you wouldn't stay with a miser like him for so long. You could have any man you wanted, even secure yourself with an advantageous marriage. No, it wasn't a simple matter of being handed a few francs every now and then that kept you by Monsieur Barbier's side. In fact, I'd venture to say you had to buy your own First Class ticket. Why else would you be in an entirely separate car?" Penelope was taking a stab with that one, but on everything else, she was almost certain.

Still, Cosette's cool, satisfied look gave Penelope pause. "You are wrong. Aristide purchased a ticket for me, as well as the compartment next to mine. I'm sure the record will confirm as much."

Adrien cleared his throat to draw attention to himself.

"It is true, Mademoiselle. Monsieur Barbier was to be in compartment 303. I handed him the key myself when he boarded in Menton. He even occupied it at the start of the journey."

The conductor didn't like him revealing that bit of information, no doubt still concerned about passenger privacy, even after everything that had happened. "That information is not to be given out, Adrien."

"I was only trying to help Mademoiselle Cochet," Adrien said helplessly.

However, Penelope noted the conductor wasn't the only one upset by the revelation. Simon and André seemed irritated as well. It only made sense now that they were here because of Monsieur Barbier. He had no doubt been killed for that reason—a reason Pen would probably never get out of them.

But someone on board knew.

She returned her attention to Cosette, who seemed even more self-satisfied. Penelope didn't think she was wrong about her, but maybe she had misunderstood the reality of Cosette's true motives.

"That begs the question of what Monsieur Barbier was doing in a compartment in the second car." Richard was the one to ask this, posing the question that everyone was now pondering.

All eyes turned to the two men who had sat at dinner with them. André and Simon seemed not only irritated but surprisingly exasperated, as though he had somehow betrayed them. Penelope turned to study Richard, thinking of something he'd said earlier.

"You're working with them!" Pen blurted out before she could stop herself. Richard, bless him, couldn't hide his surprise or his guilt.

"It isn't what you think, nothing related to this case."

Simon was quick to stop him. "Monsieur Prescott, I urge you to—"

"I think perhaps we all have a right to know exactly what the devil is going on," Thomas demanded. "A man has been murdered, after all."

"I agree," Cousin Cordelia said. "One of the people in this room is a killer. I shan't sleep a wink until we reach Paris, or at least Lyon, and he or she is arrested."

"And while we're at it, perhaps we can get some clarification on this business between Mademoiselle Cochet and Monsieur Barbier," Benny said, casting a sly look Cosette's way. Of course he'd be most interested in the tawdriest aspect.

"I'd like to know that as well," Marie said, her gaze even more castigating as it landed on Cosette. Her resentment seemed awfully personal, which made Penelope wonder if perhaps she knew Cosette as well. However, the far more glamorous blonde simply looked back at Marie with the interest one might show an ant on the ground. There was no recognition at all.

However, Penelope was at present, rather preoccupied with what her fiancé had been keeping from her. "Richard?"

"At this point, it is only right that I explain," Richard said to Simon and André.

"Please do," Pen said before either of them could protest.

"It's with regard to the Fabergé Egg."

She knew instantly to what he was referring. It did nothing to assuage her irritation. Frankly, as she'd been an integral part of the case where that Egg had disappeared (again), she saw no reason why she should have been left in the dark.

"I told you on the ship here that I had been commandeered to continue investigating where the Egg might be. Once we learned it was in Europe, it was inevitable that the International Criminal Police Commission would be involved. These two men are my liaisons."

"So this reunion of your war friends that had you leaving earlier to Paris than scheduled was a fib, I suppose."

"It was a cover, though I do still plan on meeting with them when we get to Paris." A small wrinkle formed in his brow.

"But who is to say these international police are innocent?" Honorine offered, giving Simon and André a taunting look. "I have found that police are as easily lured into temptation for sin as any other. Whatever the reason they were investigating Monsieur Barbier, it must be as valuable as a Fabergé Egg. *Très séduisante...*"

That had Simon and André protesting. The other passengers weren't to be silenced at the news, wanting to know what it was they were after. It was rather turning into a revolt.

"Please, please," the conductor shouted, silencing the room. "The murder will be resolved when the proper authorities are involved. For now, you will all be safest with everyone here in the lounge.

Simon added his own bit of warning. "As for Monsieur Barbier's accommodations or why we are on the train, I am afraid we cannot divulge that information."

"Oh, let's all stop this charade, shall we?" Lucien said, standing up. He pulled his cigarette case out and stuck one in his mouth. His brow wrinkled with consternation when he remembered he didn't have his lighter. While everyone waited with bated breath to see what he was going to reveal, he enjoyed the suspense, leisurely pulling out the matchbox instead. He selected one and lit the tip of the cigarette. He took several puffs, eyeing each person in the room before settling his gaze on Penelope. "You are right, mademoiselle, Cosette is not who she purports to be."

"Lucien!"

He laughed at Cosette's protest, ignoring her as he kept his attention on Penelope. "For that matter, neither am I."

CHAPTER EIGHTEEN

Even Penelope found herself surprised by Lucien's confession.

"Who are you, if not yourself?" Benny asked in a droll voice. He was enjoying this entirely too much.

Lucien turned to offer him an ironic smile, then he turned to Simon and André with a wicked gleam in his eye. "I was here to steal the Golden Monkey of Kashmir."

"A monkey?" Cousin Cordelia asked, her face wrinkled with confusion. It matched that of everyone else in the car—almost everyone else.

"Oh, please tell me it's a *real* monkey," Benny crooned.

"I think we'd all notice a monkey climbing the walls, even in this circus," Lulu said.

"No, not a literal monkey. Something far more valuable, priceless really," Lucien stated, casting a sly smile toward Simon and André, who looked angry, but not surprised or confused. "Of course, there is a price for everything."

"So Monsieur Barbier had this Golden Monkey and you bought a ticket hoping to steal it from him? What aren't you telling us?" Penelope asked.

"I was here to steal the monkey....back."

"I see, Monsieur Barbier stole it first," Penelope said with understanding. It was beginning to make sense now. She looked toward Cosette. "I assume you were doing the same thing. There must be some finder's fee involved."

"The reward offered is...very large," Cosette said. "A monkey made of gold with emerald eyes, made for the sultan of Kashmir in the fifteenth century. It was lost during the First Anglo-Sikh War of 1846."

"And now presumably lost once again," Penelope said. "Unless it is still in Monsieur Barbier's quarters?"

"Which quarters, is the question," Richard said.

"Certainly not the compartment in the third car," Penelope said. She gave Cosette and Lucien a sardonic look. "These two have no doubt torn that one apart in search of it. No, it would be in the compartment he conveniently had in the second car."

"Which yet again begs the question of why and how he had that compartment," Richard said.

Everyone turned to look at Simon and André, or perhaps the conductor who stood next to them, hoping for an answer.

Penelope's eyes were trained on Monsieur Padou. He had been quiet and watchful so far. He felt her gaze on him and met her with a steady look that revealed nothing.

"Compartment 204 opens to 205. That makes it awfully convenient for you to operate without witnesses, Monsieur Padou."

"We have already searched Monsieur Padou's compartment, and found nothing," André said. He turned to the man with a defiant gaze. "As part of a crime scene."

That was a tenuous argument, that would hardly hold up under scrutiny. Surely even the international police needed some sort of due process, warrant, or other form of permission to do such a thing? However, it was moot in retrospect, as they had found nothing.

The only sign that Monsieur Padou was upset by this was a slight tightening of his jaw. He otherwise remained impassive, continuing to meet Penelope with a placid stare. "Of course you haven't, as there was nothing to be found. As stated before, I did not know Monsieur Barbier, and I certainly didn't purchase a ticket to have a clandestine meeting with him. I'm sure there is a record to that effect. The second ticket was presumably bought under his own name. Perhaps he wanted to get away from other vultures on board." He slid his eyes to Lucien and Cosette.

"Did you find a suitcase?" Penelope asked, the thought suddenly coming to her.

"Pardon?" Simon asked, giving Penelope a slightly irritated look.

"In Monsieur Padou's compartment. A brown suitcase, did you see one in there?"

"Yes, why?"

Penelope felt her balloon burst, realizing her thought had led to nothing of consequence. She gave a dismissive shake of the head telling Simon he could ignore the question. However, Monsieur Padou studied her more carefully, his eyes filled with suspicion. Perhaps it was the natural reaction to someone knowing more about you than was comfortable. Perhaps it was the concern that she was onto something with him. But if the suitcase that had been left in Marseilles wasn't his, whose was it?

"Aristide had a brown suitcase. It wasn't in his compartment when I saw him...last," Cosette announced. "Did you find it in your search of his room? Perhaps in the closet or washroom?"

Simon and André glanced at one another then back to Cosette. "He had a suitcase? Can you describe it?"

"It was brown. Ordinary. Nothing remarkable. In fact, I thought it a bit dull for someone with so much money. Do you mean to say it isn't among his things?"

They didn't answer, but the sharp looks in their eyes did that for them. Both men instantly turned to Penelope. "How did you know about this suitcase?"

"I happened to see Monsieur Padou board the train with one in Cannes, just before dinner. I didn't think anything of it, until I saw the same suitcase, or what I thought was the same suitcase being taken off the train and put onto a cart in Marseilles."

"That must have been Monsieur Barbier's," Quentin said, looking rather ashen. When everyone turned to him, he paled a few more shades and swallowed hard before speaking again. "I confess, I did not know he was dead, or even that it was his when I carried it off the train."

"Explain your actions," The conductor demanded.

"It was sitting by my station in the second carriage when I returned from using the facilities. There was just an envelope with several francs and a note stating that it should be taken off the train at Marseilles and left in the luggage claims room."

"We must get a hold of that suitcase," Simon said.

"I shall contact the station now." The conductor quickly left.

Penelope surveyed the other passengers to see if any of them reacted to that news. Either they all had very good poker faces or none of them were guilty. Considering how many people in the room had done a fine job of disguising who they were and their true motives, she would have put her money on the former.

"I think it's safe to say that whoever had that suitcase removed from the train is our killer," André said, his eyes filled with accusation as they landed on everyone, even poor Cousin Cordelia.

"Before you suggest *moi*," Honorine said. "My compartment has no access to Monsieur Barbier's. I knew nothing of this Golden Monkey, and I certainly wouldn't kill for such a prize—or for a client, for that matter."

"You might if the target you were after discovered your motives? Perhaps in the act of breaking into his room? Avoiding prison, even for something so minor is a motive." Simon regarded her with renewed interest.

"As I've stated, I've been charged before," Honorine said with a dismissive wave of the hand. "The threat of prison does not frighten me."

"*Bien*, because we have searched your quarters as well."

Honorine was not quite as sedate about that as Monsieur Padou had been. "You did? Under what authority? I gave no permission!"

"We found nothing," Simon said in a dismissive voice, that all but told her to keep quiet lest they make more trouble for her.

"Who else's quarters do you plan on searching? Surely not ours? We've done nothing wrong, we don't even know Monsieur Barbier," Thomas said.

Penelope noted the way Marie briefly darted her eyes toward Lucien—who grinned back just as briefly, but quite devilishly—before focusing her attention on Thomas again. Penelope didn't need any special abilities to see that the couple not only knew Monsieur Barbier, but Lucien knew that they did. Further, they obviously had something in their rooms they didn't want Simon and André to discover.

"This discussion simply brings us back to the question

of the timeline," Richard stated. "After all, now that we know greed was a likely motive, which could be applied to any of us, including those who may have only discovered this Golden Monkey of Kashmir while on board, that leaves means and opportunity as the only way to narrow down our suspects."

"Yes," Simon agreed. "We all saw Monsieur Barbier at dinner until he returned to his quarters. From that point on, it is a matter of who may have had access to him, and whether they can prove he was alive after that. Which means we come back to you, Mademoiselle Cochet." All eyes turned to Cosette, who looked indignant. "You were the first to supposedly talk with Monsieur Barbier. The question is, was he alive when you left?"

CHAPTER NINETEEN

"Of course Aristide was alive after I talked to him!" Cosette spat, giving Simon a defiant look after his suggestion that she was the last to see him before he was murdered.

Penelope recalled that there was one other individual who had most likely interacted with Aristide Barbier before Cosette did. Monsieur Padou was the first to leave the dining room, even before Aristide did. However, Simon was right to start with Cosette as she was the only one who had claimed to actually speak with him.

"But your instructions regarding his dinner, you insisted that the tray be delivered and set outside of his compartment with nothing more than a knock on the door," André said. "You claimed he did not want to be disturbed."

"That is what he told me!"

"Did he tell you *why* he did not want to return to dinner?" André's voice was filled with skepticism.

"I knocked and opened the door before he could respond. He had the Golden Monkey on the table wrapping it in some cloth. He was quite angry when he realized I had seen it. I assume he didn't want any further trespassers intruding on him, including Quentin. He told me to have his dinner sent to his accommodations and that the person who brought it shouldn't expect him to open the door. He made sure to lock it when he closed the door in my face. But he was alive!"

Simon turned to Quentin. "Did Monsieur Barbier say anything when you returned with the tray? Did you see him open the door and take the tray in?"

"Yes. I left the tray outside of his door, with a knock and a word to let him know it was there. When I returned to my station at the end of the car, I saw his door open, and he reached out to pull in his tray of food."

"So he was alive! I am not the killer," Cosette said, looking more relieved than anything.

Simon frowned at her, then turned it on Marie and Thomas. "The two of you left before Quentin returned with the tray, rather abruptly, I might add. Explain your actions. Perhaps you knew the car would be empty?"

"We had no reason to talk to Monsieur Barbier," Thomas said with a sneer, spitting out his name. "How would we have even known about this supposed Golden Monkey? For that matter, why would we have killed him? As you have just confirmed, he was alive when Quentin returned with the tray. We were sat at our table by the time he opened his door to collect his dinner."

"That does not prove your innocence, nor does it explain why you left during dinner. There has been something very suspicious about the two of you. The murder could have just as easily happened later on in the evening, perhaps when Quentin was otherwise occupied?" Simon glanced at Quentin with a warning look, perhaps telling him not to reveal exactly when he was away from his station during the course of the evening.

"Which means that woman is not necessarily innocent either," Marie accused, shooting daggers at Cosette. "It was not enough for him to spend his money on you—money that was not even his—you wanted even more. Why settle for a First Class ticket or even a *supposed* finder's fee when you could have a fortune? Never mind how many people are hurt in the process...or killed."

"*Marie*," Thomas said sternly enough to arrest her attention, then added in a softer voice, "that is enough."

"How dare you," Cosette cried, looking surprisingly wounded. "My only goal was to return the Golden Monkey to its rightful owner, that is all. I would never kill for such a thing."

"But would you share a bed for such a thing?" Lucien offered, his eyes intensely trained on her.

Penelope wouldn't have been surprised if she got up from her chair just to slap him, at that point. Instead, she seemed to collect herself, ignoring him, before continuing.

"The point remains, many others in this room had means and opportunity to kill Aristide. Someone in this room was the last to see him alive, but that was not me." Cosette fell back into her chair and pointedly turned her attention to the window as though she was done defending herself.

Everyone in the car was focused on Cosette, but Penelope was still pondering the supposedly newlywed couple. Simon was correct in suggesting that they were also not all they appeared. She decided to address the one thing that stuck out the most in terms of what was bothering her.

"Why did the two of you purchase two separate compartments?"

Thomas and Marie turned to her in surprise.

"What does that matter?" Thomas insisted. "That is hardly suspicious."

"I wouldn't say that. You are a newlywed couple, and it is a simple overnight trip. Why would you spend such a large amount for two compartments? I would think that a couple free to...*entertain* all that marriage had to offer without fear of public scrutiny would indulge in such an opportunity. Particularly if it meant saving money."

It was subtle, but Penelope noted their reaction at the suggestion she had made about sharing a compartment. Thomas grimaced with distaste and his nose wrinkled ever so slightly, as though smelling something foul. Marie edged away from his embrace, as though she wanted a clear barrier between them.

"Ah," Penelope said with sudden understanding. "You aren't really married."

"Why would anyone pretend to be newlyweds?" Cousin Cordelia asked, scandalized that anyone would do such a thing.

"Perhaps we simply don't advertise what married couples do in the privacy of their own home. Unlike some, we do have a certain sense of propriety," Thomas said, giving Penelope and Richard a scathing sneer before adding, "even those who have yet to take their vows."

Before Penelope could respond, Honorine laughed lightly. "Deflection is the calling card of deceit, *mon ami*."

"Not you as well," Thomas said with exasperation. "Another woman with questionable morals. One might be left wondering how your husband actually died?"

"No need to wonder," Honorine said in a breezy tone. "He was old and frail. Why do you suppose I married him in the first place?"

Thomas coughed out a sharp laugh, as though that explained enough.

"But I did not kill him, *and* I was in fact married to him."

"This is absurd," Marie said, though she did wriggle out from beneath Thomas's arm around her shoulder to get even further away from him. "Our marriage is not at issue, presently. That woman having every reason to steal and then commit murder is." She pointed at Cosette, but it did no good. Everyone had been drawn in by the scandalous proposition that Marie and Thomas were not the husband and wife they purported to be.

"You have nothing but speculation to go on," Thomas insisted, sounding desperate.

"There are signs, if one looks closely," Penelope said. She nodded towards Marie. "I'm afraid you are the most obvious one." The way Marie's hand went up to her hair all but cinched it. "There, that is one indication. I've rarely seen hair that color in anyone older than five. It's about as natural as Mademoiselle Cochet's."

The only indication that Cosette was upset about this was a short exhale of laughter.

"And the makeup you wore at dinner. It was…well it is not something that comes naturally to you, I suspect. You applied it with a rather heavy hand, I'm afraid. It's a direct contrast to the slightly old-fashioned dress you're wearing. Well, more *old* than old-fashioned, I suppose. The same one you wore at dinner. Most women your age have inched their hemlines higher these days. That is unless they are overly modest or they can't afford modern fashion. In your case, I suspect the latter. No one who is in any way prudish would wear that much rouge."

"Are you suggesting I am a woman of ill repute?" Marie was indignant.

Penelope tilted her head. "No, particularly since you refrained from putting any makeup on before joining us tonight. Honestly, I don't know why you even bothered at dinner, your natural face is quite pretty. You don't need makeup. It makes me wonder why there isn't a speck of it on now."

"So not wearing makeup is a crime?"

"It's the middle of the night and we're all in shock from the murder," Thomas argued.

"It's a rare woman who doesn't at least do a little something to put herself together before joining company. If you look closely at most of the women in this room, you'll see we have dabbed a bit of something on, even yours truly."

"So now she is a suspect simply because she doesn't paint herself like a harlot?" Thomas scoffed.

"Well...yes."

Thomas and Marie blinked in surprise.

"Penelope!" Cousin Cordelia exclaimed in admonishment.

"Now, now, I think the scorn is reserved for Madame Smith," Honorine said, walking closer to the couple. "Or should I say Mademoiselle?"

"I suspect the heavy makeup was because you didn't want someone on this train to recognize you, correct? There is only one person who is no longer with us," Penelope said, drawing the couple's attention again. "And it is obvious even the mention of marriage between the two of you fills you with revulsion. Because you're brother and sister, not husband and wife. The similarities in features are there. Particularly if Marie hadn't dyed her hair blonde."

"I beg your pardon?" Thomas said, lifting his chin even higher. "How dare you suggest—"

"Edward, please." Marie seemed almost relieved.

"Edward is it?" Honorine said with a broad smile. She held out her hand to him. "A pleasure to meet you...finally."

He looked down at Honorine's hand with contempt, then turned it on the woman next to him, warning her not to speak any further.

She ignored him as she continued her confession. "Yes, he is my brother, Edward. My name isn't Marie, it's Margaret, Margaret Stillman. We did board this train in hopes of confronting Aristide Barbier, but we did not kill him!"

"I think you had better tell us everything," Simon insisted.

Edward still seemed reluctant, but Margaret was eager to relieve herself of the burden of secrecy. "Aristide Barbier swindled our mother out of the money our father had left to her. He claimed to be an international financial advisor, investing in a bit of land ripe for development in a particular area of Provence. Mother has always been enamored of France, and he made it sound exciting and romantic. Our father had always handled the money, and when he died, she was vulnerable and frankly, quite financially illiterate. She..." Margaret cast a quick, uncomfortable look toward her brother, who remained stone-faced, "resisted any offers of assistance from Edward."

Penelope didn't need to be a private investigator to discover why that was. Edward had probably offered his help as tactfully as a bull charging a matador. Even a woman who knew she needed such help would not allow her pride to accept it. Margaret confirmed as much.

"Mother and Edward have been estranged for some time now, you see."

"For heaven's sake, Margaret, they don't need to know everything."

"I'm only attempting to explain things, Edward," she said, then turned to the rest of them. "It was to the point that mother had put away any photos of him...but not any of me. I knew this man had been to her home, and thus seen photos of me, so that is why I attempted to disguise myself with makeup and a change of hair."

Edward finished for her. "It was only when a family friend reached out to inform us that mother had been borrowing money from him simply to pay her bills that she finally revealed what had happened. She is about to lose her home, the home we were raised in. We were desperate. I can't fathom why he would have gone after someone with so little to her name in the first place. I was left some stock shares, which I sold to hire a private investigator to learn more about who this man had been. Naturally, he went by a different name in his meetings with our mother. Recently, we discovered his real identity and his whereabouts in the south of France. I brought Margaret to maintain a ruse of being a married couple, which was less suspicious. We arrived in Menton just in time to learn he was heading to Paris via this train, so we bought two tickets for ourselves. The splurge seemed worth it, if only to get Mother's money back."

Now the resentful looks Margaret had cast Cosette's way made sense. It wasn't envy or jealousy, at least not in the way Penelope had first assumed. She had no doubt been thinking of the money Aristide was spending on his pretty young companion, money that had been swindled from her mother. Pen turned to Honorine. It seemed Monsieur

Barbier made a habit of relieving women of their fortunes, even his own wife.

"You do realize this makes you a suspect," Simon said, though with sympathy in his voice. "I must insist you tell us why you left during dinner."

The two looked at one another before Margaret spoke first.

"We had planned on confronting him after dinner. When Mademoiselle Cochet stated he would not be returning, Edward became impatient. I left, only to keep him from doing anything drastic."

"But we did not kill him!" Edward insisted. "I can tell you for a fact that he was still in his compartment and very much alive when we returned to the dining room."

Something about that answer struck Penelope. It took her only a moment to realize what bothered her about it, most notably when her eyes wandered toward Margaret. That's when she knew what it was they weren't telling everyone.

CHAPTER TWENTY

"How do you know Monsieur Barbier was in his compartment when you left?" Penelope asked.

Edward and Margaret, formerly known as Thomas and Marie, both turned to her with frowns.

"We..." Margaret began, but Edward quickly interrupted her.

"We know because we didn't kill him. Where would he otherwise be?"

"Yes, but you specifically stated he was in his compartment. How do you know for sure?"

"It's simply a matter of phrasing. What does it really matter?" Edward was becoming agitated. "As I stated, where else would he be?"

"You went to confront him, presumably that might involve knocking on his door? Did he answer or not?"

Rather than give a straight response, Edward and Margaret glanced at one another, which was a mistake.

"Perhaps you took it upon yourself to enter?" Penelope suggested.

"That is preposterous!" Edward's face was now red with indignation.

"Did you or did you not enter Monsieur Barbier's compartment? It is a yes or no answer," André, the more temperamental of the two police, demanded.

"How could we have possibly done that?"

"Ah, monsieur, that was not an answer," Honorine stated in a slightly taunting voice.

"They did," Penelope finally said, ending the interrogation.

"How do you know that?" Edward spat, glaring at her.

"Margaret's third bobby pin. It was missing when you returned to dinner. She had three before you left, and only two upon returning. I suspect it was ruined when you picked the lock for compartment 204." The way Margaret's hand inadvertently rose to glance across her hair, told Penelope her suspicion had been correct. Goodness, the poor woman would have been hopeless in a game of poker. "If you are smart, you will have gotten rid of it. Then again, it may be the proof you need to confirm your story...your *real* story."

"Perhaps it is time you told us the *real* story," Simon said, pinning them with a gaze indicating he would tolerate no more lies.

Margaret touched Edward's arm and he seemed to relent. He sighed, closed his eyes, and then spoke. "Margaret is correct, we intended to confront Aristide after dinner. Then Cosette came in and made the announcement that he would be remaining in his compartment. When Quentin entered the dining room, we thought perhaps there was an opportunity to confront him with a bit of privacy. We simply wanted our mother's money returned, that is all! At most, we planned on threatening legal consequences, certainly not murder. We knocked but there was no answer. I assumed he was being stubborn. After all, we could smell his cigarette even there in the corridor, so we knew he was in there."

So that had been the cause of the cigarette smoke lingering in the second compartment. Penelope recalled Aristide smoking a cigarette in the lounge after his wallet had been returned. Lucien wasn't the only smoker on board.

"It...it angered me," Edward continued, his face contorted with frustration. "It was as though he was taunting us with his silence. Margaret suggested we try our hand at picking the lock. We aren't experts, mind you. Honestly, we were both surprised when it actually worked. We managed to get the door unlocked, but of course that is when *Monsieur Barbier*," he spat the name, "decided to respond to us. He pushed back against the door, preventing us from entering. He closed it shut and locked it once again. We saw Quentin returning and didn't make another attempt to enter. I should remind you, he *has* stated that he saw Aristide retrieve the tray of food after we had gone. He was alive!"

Penelope considered this. It was odd someone like Aristide wouldn't have let his outrage be known. "Did he say anything at all when you managed to unlock the door?"

"Just a grunt of surprise. Then, once the door was closed, he said 'how dare you.' Fortunately, he didn't say anything further by the time Quentin arrived."

"And it was his voice? You're sure of it?"

"Yes, he was understandably quite angry, but it was him."

"So, if you are telling the truth, he was alive when you returned to dinner," Simon said.

"You never entered the compartment?" André confirmed

"We didn't even get the door open wide enough to so much as peek inside."

Simon turned to Quentin. "Did Monsieur Barbier mention this incident to you at all?"

Quentin shook his head. "No, I knocked and left the tray as instructed. He said nothing when he opened the door and took it."

"Well, he wouldn't have wanted you or anyone else to see what he had been up to with the Golden Monkey. He would have avoided any sort of investigation, I imagine," Simon surmised.

"If that blasted Golden Monkey *had* been there, I see no reason why it shouldn't have been ours to take." Edward's bravado faltered a bit when his eyes darted to Simon and André, who most certainly disagreed with that declaration if their expressions were any indication. "However, as stated, we never even managed to look in the compartment."

"You can search our compartments if you think we are lying," Margaret insisted. "Our only aim was to recover the money taken from our mother. Now that everything is out in the open, we have nothing more to hide."

Edward nodded. "Exactly. Anything we may have done that wasn't exactly above reproach was done with the most honest intentions. We had no reason to kill Aristide, not before we got our money back. As it is, we may never see a pound of it."

During Edward's exposition, Penelope studied the other passengers in the car. Cosette seemed relieved, but intrigued. Lucien tried to seem only casually interested, but his eyes were sharp with interest. Honorine simply seemed amused as usual. The bartender was rapt with attention, no doubt experiencing the most interesting night during his tenure with the train company. As for the three concierges, Quentin seemed worried about possibly losing his job, Adrien simply looked overwhelmed, and Jules, the only concierge whose charges weren't likely murderers or thieves, maintained his professional dignity.

However, it was Monsieur Padou that Penelope found most curious. He remained politely interested at most, his fingers lightly tapping on his oversized book. It still bothered her that his compartment just happened to be next to Aristide Barbier's—a man who had for some reason reserved two compartments. Without anything beyond simply having the same suitcase, there was no way to confirm that he even knew Monsieur Barbier.

Monsieur Padou once again sensed Penelope studying him and he returned the same unreadable look. Perhaps it was her suspicious imagination, but she could have sworn there was a hint of smugness there, as though he was daring her to find any evidence of his involvement in the murder or theft. Honestly, it was rather odd that so many fellow First Class passengers had interests that involved Monsieur Barbier. That thought derailed her interest in Monsieur Padou.

She turned to Edward and Margaret. "How did you just happen to know Monsieur Barbier was going to be on this train?"

"A telegram was sent to me, several weeks ago," Margaret said. "I have it in my compartment. It told me that the man Edward and I were looking for would be in Menton, boarding this very train."

So, that was what she had really been worried about

Simon and André finding during a search. Now that the true motives of Margaret and her brother were revealed, it no longer mattered.

"I too received a telegram," Honorine said, then frowned in annoyance. "Of course, mine indicated I should board in Monte Carlo."

That left the car in stunned silence. Someone had been working behind the scenes to ensure that multiple interested parties were on the same train as Aristide Barbier—all of them with an ulterior motive. Was it perhaps a Good Samaritan helping those who'd been wronged? Or was it to provide multiple suspects to distract from the real killer?

Penelope turned to Simon and André. "Don't you find it odd that so many people in First Class just happen to be very interested in Monsieur Barbier and just happened to receive a telegram telling them they should be on this train? At least those who have confessed to it." She cast another narrow-eyed look Monsieur Padou's way before continuing. "I assume you and Monsieur Robineau have been following him for a while and knew about his tickets as soon as he purchased them. The same is understandable for Mademoiselle Cochet. However, the others, I'm quite puzzled by the coincidence."

"I suppose I should confess myself, innocent as a lamb that I am," Lucien said with a sly smile. "I simply followed the lovely Miss Cochet...though, I had to first learn her *nom de guerre*." He gave her a wink.

"An unwelcome surprise." Cosette glared at Lucien, then turned her attention to the rest of the room. "If you're hoping for my real name you won't get it. However, I received a letter telling me about the Golden Monkey and offering me an opportunity to make a good deal of reward money. I was told I would find him in Menton, and I did. I used my charms to seduce him so I could get close enough to discover where it was. Why would I invite so many obstacles to my goal? As it is, I am innocent of killing him *and* of stealing the Golden Monkey, as all of this nonsense continues to prove. Aristide was alive when I left during dinner service—without the Golden Monkey! After that, I was in the third carriage, at least until I discovered he had been murdered."

"As was I," Lucien added. "So fortuitous that I managed a ticket for myself...so close to such loveliness."

"Er..." Adrien began, then quickly thought better of it.

"If you have something to say, speak," André insisted.

"Do you have information regarding Monsieur Vollant?" Simon asked, his brow furrowed.

Adrien looked as though he regretted uttering anything. He cast a worried look to Lucien, then to Simon. Pen took a moment to consider why he would be so worried, then it struck her. Honorine had earlier indicated she had purchased the last ticket for First Class. So how had Lucien been so lucky? And why had that third car been so empty?

"Well, go on," Simon urged.

"Lucien stole the ticket," Penelope said, giving Lucien a harsh look. "From a family, I might add. Shame on you." She turned to Simon and André. "There was a family of five on the platform, a husband and wife, two small girls, and an older boy. They would have purchased three compartments to accommodate them all. The mother and father were arguing, presumably over the lost tickets."

Lucien sported a wounded expression. "I am offended you think so lowly of me, Mademoiselle Banks."

"It is true!" Adrien finally sputtered. "When I inquired about it, as he did not match the names I had on my list of passengers for the third carriage, he told me the family had sold him the tickets. I did not question it, as he had a ticket in hand."

Penelope figured there had also probably been an exchange of several francs to not make a fuss about it. She decided not to address it as the poor concierge already looked devastated, particularly under the withering look Simon and André gave him.

"So, you claim you tailed Cosette. Why steal tickets from a family in Nice instead of Menton?" Richard asked.

Lucien simply stared back with a grin, as though it was a riddle that they needed to solve. Penelope considered the man in question, one who had no scruples, could be quite charming, and wasn't above greasing a few palms if need be.

"You bribed someone to get the passenger list and which compartment they would be in. You learned Monsieur Barbier had a ticket in the third carriage, which is where you assumed he would be staying. The only other passengers in that car were Cosette and the family boarding in Nice. Thus, you quickly drove to Nice to beat the train and liberate the poor family of their pre-purchased tickets."

Lucien laughed, then shrugged as though that were no great matter. Considering the cost of the tickets, Penelope thought the family might beg to disagree. Simon and André sported looks of disapproval, as did many of the other passengers.

"So who was listed for Monsieur Barbier's compartment in the second carriage?" Richard asked.

All eyes turned to the trio of concierges. Quentin was the one to answer. "It was a Jaques Arsenault, originally."

Margaret gasped in surprise.

At the same time, Cosette coughed out a sharp laugh. She looked around with incredulity, then turned back to Quentin. "And you simply gave Aristide this room?"

"Did you say Jaques Arsenault?" Edward demanded.

"Oui," Quentin said, then turned to Cosette to answer her question. "There was an update in Monte Carlo. The ticket had been transferred to Monsieur Barbier. That is when he took possession of it. I alerted my fellow concierges and the conductor." He gestured to Simon and André, who did not seem surprised.

However, they, like almost everyone else, were focused on Edward and Margaret.

"The name Jaques Arsenault, it means something to you?"

"That is the name he used with our mother," Edward said.

André cursed under his breath in French. "How did we not know this alias?"

"That is a good question," Simon said with a frown.

Penelope had to agree with him. Surely they did their research prior to boarding the train. It seemed this was an alias Aristide Barbier liked to use on more than one occasion, at least when he was partaking in his misdeeds. Which begged the question as to which misdeed he was partaking in during this train ride?

"It seems you were correct in your claim that he purchased the ticket himself, Monsieur Padou," Penelope remarked. "It still remains an interesting coincidence that he picked a room that just happens to open to yours."

Monsieur Padou simply stared back with a blithe expression of disinterest. "I applaud your talent for creating intrigue, Mademoiselle Banks. Sadly, I must, once again, disappoint. My room has been searched, though without permission," he cast a brief sour look toward Simon and André. "Unless you think perhaps I am carrying this stolen monkey on my person, there is no further reason to cast such accusations my way."

Penelope frowned at him casually tapping one finger against his book, that smug look still on his face. It was there somewhere, she just needed the connection.

Then it came to her. "It was a trade. That's what this entire train ride has been about!"

CHAPTER TWENTY-ONE

It was clear from the expressions on everyone's face that they had no idea what Penelope was talking about, so she repeated herself.

"It was a trade," Pen said, gesturing toward Monsieur Padou's book. "The Golden Monkey for the book."

She was a bit thrown by the way Monsieur Padou's mouth quirked on one side, as though she was, yet again, going down the wrong path.

"If it was a trade, this book for that monkey, then why do I still have the book in my possession? Furthermore, why do I *not* have the Golden Monkey in my possession?"

"Because you stole it," Penelope said with exasperation. "You're the one who put it in the suitcase and had it sent to the station. I'm certain you were hoping to collect it once you disembarked from the train. That is why there was no name attached to the suitcase."

Still, he did not seem the slightest bit perturbed, which only created further doubt in Penelope's mind. The other passengers looked skeptical, even her own friends.

"I'm afraid I may have given you the wrong impression

earlier about the value of this book, my dear," Monsieur Padou said, patting the cover. "Yes, it is fairly rare, but hardly worth a fortune equivalent to that of a gold figurine with emerald eyes. I *did* say it was a reproduction, but even if I had been lying about that, a real first edition of this text would only fetch about a hundred francs, at most. Any rare book dealer will tell you."

"Monsieur Padou—pardon, what is your full name?" Simon asked.

"Pierre Padou."

"May we see this book for ourselves?"

Monsieur Padou pursed his lips with mild reluctance, which seemed mostly to make a point, but he finally acquiesced. Simon quickly took the book, struggling to hold it in his hands as he flipped through the pages. André looked over his shoulder, his nose wrinkled as he tried to decipher what was so special about the book. Finally both of them looked up and met Penelope with frowns of confusion.

"I see nothing strange about this book." Simon said as he handed it back to the smug Pierre.

"It might help if you had at least something more than supposition, Penelope," Richard offered.

Pen felt a slight sense of betrayal, but he was right. All she had was accusations to offer. She needed something solid to make those accusations stick.

Stick...

"That's it!" Penelope said, her eyes brightening. She turned to André in particular. "You smelled it just now, a scent of glue? That's why your nose was wrinkled."

André frowned. "Oui, but what does that prove?"

"The pages, they're very thick. That's because they've been glued together. Either that, or the lining of the interior. That's where he kept the money or some other form of payment. The payment he never gave to Monsieur Barbier, or perhaps stole back from him...after he killed him. Why not put it into the same book from which it was transported onto the train?"

"There *was* glue found in his compartment," Simon said.

"Give me that book," André demanded, reaching for it.

"I do not give you permission!" Monsieur Padou protested, pressing his hand down on the book. "You have no authority to simply seize property and potentially destroy it, all on the claim of some mad woman who reads too many detective novels."

Suddenly everyone was alert. He had all but confessed to his crime by his refusal. The way his face paled and beads of sweat began to appear on his brow only confirmed it. After being so smugly silent and seemingly innocent, he now looked mildly panicked. Penelope couldn't help but feel justified in her accusations.

Simon only laughed softly. "We are placing you under arrest, Monsieur Padou. All items in your possession are free to be searched, but I do not think we need to do that here. Once you are taken in, we will search the book more thoroughly."

"That's why Monsieur Barbier had the letter opener, which Monsieur Padou used to kill him," Penelope said, unable to stop herself from continuing her accusations now that she had been proven right. "There were no letters in his room. He used it to separate the pages and retrieve what is hidden between them."

"No! That is not true, I did not kill him."

André sneered with derision. "Of course you would say that now."

Pierre closed his eyes and exhaled, calming down. "It is

true, there are bearer bonds in between the pages of this book. That is not a crime, as they are mine."

"It is a crime to buy stolen property," Cosette accused.

"Except there was no stolen property to be had," he spat back.

"What does that mean?" André demanded.

"Please explain," Simon said, placing a calming hand on his more tempestuous partner, who seemed ready to lock up Pierre and throw away the key.

Pierre seemed reluctant to say anything at first, but he relented, realizing that it might be his only avenue to avoid a murder charge. "Via certain...*connections*, I discovered the Golden Monkey of Kashmir was available from an interested seller. Contact was made, and a point of sale suggested. I wasn't about to buy from an unknown dealer without doing my investigation before hand. His wife, for one, was in search of him and the money he had apparently disappeared with. It was not a surprise to find she had hired someone to search for him." He turned toward Honorine who simply lowered her eyelids in acknowledgment. "There were other people in his past, mostly older, widowed, and easily seduced or deceived women. For example, the mother of these two, now that I know their real names." He gestured toward Edward and Margaret. "I was quite surprised to find several of those interested parties sharing the train with Monsieur Barbier, though I doubt he was aware."

"So you knew who we were?" Margaret asked.

"Madame DuBois, yes. As was stated, she has a reputation in Paris." Honorine seemed tickled by the statement. "I suspected you and your brother had an ulterior motive, despite the guise as a married couple. This was confirmed by your sudden disappearance at dinner, though I wasn't sure which of his many victims you might have been. Your original names were unfamiliar to me." A thin smile spread his lips. "Monsieur Barbier, I'm afraid, left quite a trail of wronged individuals in his wake."

"This does not prove anything, I'm afraid," Simon said.

"As it happens, the deal did *not* in fact proceed as agreed upon. It was not the real Golden Monkey he traded me. It was a forgery, which I discovered soon after I returned from dinner service."

Cosette inhaled sharply. Lucien leaned in as though uncertain he had heard correctly. Simon and André looked at each other with alarm.

"Of course you would claim that. You are probably hoping that we will forgo seizing that suitcase in Marseilles." André was quite skeptical at the claim.

"Is there any way you can prove what he gave you was a forgery?" Simon demanded.

Monsieur Padou gave him a look of disdain. "I know the weight of gold, monsieur. It is heavy, even heavier than whatever the fake was made of, used as a base from which to coat it in gold, hoping to fool me. Even the emeralds were not real." He coughed out a sharp laugh at the gall. "They were far easier to spot as paste."

"Im afraid that only provides you with motive, *mon ami*," Simon said, shaking his head, though it was obvious from his wrinkled brow and taut jaw that he was still concerned about having wasted time chasing after a stolen artifact that may not have been the real thing.

"You are correct, except someone else got to Monsieur Barbier before me."

"So you claim," André said, still not convinced.

"It is true." Monsieur Padou paused in consideration before continuing. "We were to trade during dinner, making our excuses for leaving. Yes, the rooms were conjoined for that very reason. We made the trade through our connecting doors, away from prying eyes. It *was* the real Golden Monkey that I first received. In return, I gave him the book with the bonds between the pages. Only, as stated, when I returned from dinner, I found the real Golden Monkey had been replaced by a fake."

"So Monsieur Barbier did bring the real Golden Monkey with him on the train?" Simon confirmed, a look of relief on his face.

"Yes, though where it is presently, I do not know."

"And yet, you have the book of bonds that you supposedly traded for it," André pointed out.

"True. After the trade, I put the real Golden Monkey in a lock box in my suitcase before returning to dinner. I should have realized a fair trade would not be enough for him. It seems his illicit skills also translated into picking locks. At the very least, there was no way for him to escape the train if he stole the artifact back from me. Thus, when I discovered his bit of deception, I tried the door between our compartments, ready to insist on a return of my bonds."

"And killed him when he did not comply," André accused.

"No," Pierre said, giving him a patient look. "I was armed with far more effective ammunition, information. I had every intention of telling him there were many people who had a particular interest in him, at least one of whom was on board with us." He glanced at Honorine. "I planned on giving at least Madame DuBois all the information I had gathered should he have been...difficult. The door was, surprisingly, still unlocked. I found Aristide already dead in his compartment." He sighed. "Naturally, I knew I would be a suspect, as both our rooms were adjoining and at the time, unlocked. Fortunately, Quentin was away from his station at the time and there were no other passengers in the hallway. So, I took my book back, making sure the bonds were still between the pages, I locked the door opening to my room, then exited into the corridor from his compartment. I slipped back into my own room, making sure to lock my door to his compartment as well. I did not kill him. I only took back what rightfully belonged to me."

"A likely story," Edward said.

"What reason would I have had to kill him? He would not have raised a fuss, not with so many witnesses. I should say, neither of you were very subtle either." He gave Simon and André pointed looks. "I had my suspicions as to who you were as well."

"This would have been after dinner, I presume. I too noticed Quentin was not at his station," Penelope said, glancing at the concierge.

"I was with them," Quentin protested, pointing to Simon and André. "They held me for some time with their questions. We were instructed to comply with their demands."

"He alerted Jules and myself about his absence in case any of his passengers needed something," Adrien assured her.

"That means, unless Monsieur Padou is lying—"

"Which is still a possibility," André interjected.

Simon glanced at him before continuing. "—we are back to the presumption that everyone here is a suspect." He turned to Penelope and her friends. "Even you, I'm afraid."

CHAPTER TWENTY-TWO

The air in the train car was suddenly ripe with suspense. Everyone eyed one another, wondering who was the killer, now that the window of opportunity had been extended past the dinner service.

"Oh for heaven's sake, it wasn't any of my friends nor me," Penelope said to Simon at the suggestion they were also suspects, given the timeline. She gave Cosette a sharp look. "Despite the claim of others."

"Richard, dear, tell them we aren't criminals," Cousin Cordelia insisted.

"I think it's fair to say that we aren't at the top of the list of suspects," Richard said as diplomatically as possible.

Low laughter escaped from Lucien. "Oh, like the lovely Widow DuBois, I've known a few members of the law enforcement persuasion who were all too happy to dabble on the other side of the legal line." He shot Richard, then André and Simon wicked grins. He turned to give Cousin Cordelia an even more devilish one. "Not to mention seemingly innocent older madames."

"Oh." Cousin Cordelia breathed out, then frowned at him with indignation.

"So long as that means we get to stay here for the merry-go-round of interrogations, add me to the list," Benny said before pursing his lips with delight.

"Benny, really," Cousin Cordelia scolded.

"Yes, Benny, *really*," Lulu said, arching a brow in admonishment.

Honorine simply breathed out a laugh and sipped her champagne.

"Fine then, we are *all* suspects," Penelope said with impatience. "However, it behooves you to focus on those who are *most likely* to have committed the crime, does it not?"

"I wouldn't say that," Richard countered. "You know better than anyone, sometimes the least likely candidate is the guilty party."

Pen turned in surprise. Usually, he was the voice of reason, tempering her tendency to take flights of fancy with regard to guilty parties.

"However," he continued at her wounded look. "I do think plausibility cannot be ignored. I would be willing to state unequivocally that, prior to boarding this train, neither you nor anyone else in our party even knew about this Golden Monkey of Kashmir or Monsieur Barbier, for that matter." He rolled his eyes to Simon and André and frowned. "Though it would have been nice to be alerted as a professional courtesy."

"I apologize, detective, we were not at liberty to divulge any information about it," Simon said.

"Even when you knew my fiancée and friends would also be taking this train?" There was a strong undercurrent of anger in Richard's voice.

Penelope admired his desire to protect her and her friends, but she was more curious than anything. "This International Criminal Police Commission has you working on two cases at once. It must be understaffed or else it doesn't deem either to be of great importance. It's no wonder you have involved my fiancé."

André glared at her. "We do not need the opinions of civilians to tell us how to do our—"

Simon put a calming hand on his partner's shoulder. "You are correct, Mademoiselle Banks. The International Criminal Police Commission is fairly new, only established three years ago; very new, but very necessary, as both this case and that of your missing Egg have proven. I assure you, the Commission takes both cases very seriously."

"Yet you didn't even know any of Monsieur Barbier's aliases?"

"We only took charge of this case quite recently. The news of the Golden Monkey appearing on the open market was only discovered within the past month or so. It took even longer to learn who was selling it. If it had been up to me, I would have advised against combining investigations." He cast a very brief irritated glance to André, who ignored him. "Some are more ambitious at this game than they should be."

"As it is, you must be included in our list of suspects," André said, daring Penelope to challenge him. When she didn't he nodded, then his gaze traveled around the room. "Of course, your detective fiancé is correct, there are other more likely suspects."

Penelope was curious about something. "What happened to the Golden Monkey?"

"Which one?" Richard asked.

"Well...both?" She turned to Pierre. "What did you do with the fake one after you reclaimed your book?"

A small smile curled his lips. "I placed it right back on the table next to his body. It seemed rather fitting at the time."

"Oh my," Cousin Cordelia said, fanning herself at that mental image.

"I think, if you are going to keep us here as suspects, we should be allowed another drink," Honorine said, giving Pen's cousin a look of sympathy, then lifting her empty glass. Without waiting for permission, she walked to the bar and held it toward the bartender. He glanced at Simon and André for permission, and received a resigned nod from the former. That had Lucien hopping up from his chair to also refill his glass. The poor concierges looked like they could have used a drink as well.

"Did you see the brown suitcase while you were there?" Penelope asked, ignoring the rush for drinks. His answer would be telling.

"*Oui*, it was on the floor next to the couch." He gave her a knowing look. "And it was there when I left. I was not the one to have it removed from the train."

André still looked skeptical. "So, someone killed Monsieur Barbier, then came back later to steal his suitcase and, presumably, the real Golden Monkey?"

"Or, presumably, the fake one," Penelope pointed out. "After all, neither of them were in Monsieur Barbier's room when the rest of us discovered his body, at least not out in the open."

"Why take a fake one?" Simon asked.

"Perhaps the thief did not know it was fake. If Monsieur Barbier did bring two Golden Monkeys, one real and one fake, the only one who might have known that is Monsieur

Padou, and him only after noting the weight difference between the two."

"*If* he is telling the truth," André said, narrowing his gaze at him, pressing the large book closer to his chest.

Pierre was apparently done defending himself. He sat with a look on his face that almost hinted at boredom from the assault of accusations.

"It could have been two different people. One who killed him and one who took the Golden Monkey," Richard pointed out.

"And a third who took the other Golden Monkey," Pen said thoughtfully. That was certainly a lot of activity for such tight windows of time. There was the period when Quentin was retrieving Aristide's dinner, then when he was with the two international police officers.

"We must find out what was in that suitcase," Simon said. He pierced Quentin with a gaze. "Did you look in the suitcase before taking it off the train?"

Quentin was rightfully offended by the question. "Of course not."

Simon studied him for a few seconds longer then relented with a sigh. "I will go and speak to the conductor. Perhaps he has made contact with the station at Marseilles and they have retrieved the suitcase."

He left, and André remained behind, pinning everyone in the car with a hard stare lest they should make trouble for him in his partner's temporary absence. It didn't take long for Simon to return with the conductor, both of them sporting grim looks.

"Well?" Cosette demanded. "Did they apprehend the suitcase?"

Simon and the conductor glanced at one another before the former answered the question.

"The suitcase has been held and it was opened by the local authorities. After a bit of back and forth via telegram, we learned that there was only one Golden Monkey in the suitcase. It is too early to have found an expert who can confirm if it is real or fake."

"Which means the real one could still be on board," André confirmed.

Simon nodded. "That is indeed a possibility."

CHAPTER TWENTY-THREE

The news that the real Golden Monkey of Kashmir could still be on the train once again shifted the atmosphere in the room. A mixture of suspicion and, no doubt, greed seemed to infuse the air.

Penelope turned to Richard and asked in a lower tone, "Do you think it was two different people, the theft and the murder?"

"One would have to assume Monsieur Padou is telling the truth. The same is true of everyone else here. Sadly, it seems lying and deceit have been the theme of this voyage."

"True. Still, if we assume they are all telling the truth, I would think two people who have made a living recapturing stolen goods for insurance companies would also know the proper weight of the real piece. They too might have figured out which was a fake. I think the suspect list might be narrowed by the determination of whether that Golden Monkey found in the suitcase is real or not. It is a shame they haven't yet been able to determine."

"I'm happy to leave that bit to the two men from the International Criminal Police Commission. It's the murder that has me concerned. Once someone has resorted to killing, even in a fit of anger, greed, or passion, it's easier to do it again, say to keep from being discovered." He made sure to give Penelope a pointed look.

She returned a pert smile. "As you stated, I have the two men from the International Criminal Police Commission here, as well as a bona fide member of the NYPD. I feel perfectly safe," she said sweetly. She turned to see Lulu and Benny on either side of Cousin Cordelia, consoling her. Pen had a sense some small part of her cousin was thoroughly enthralled with the excitement of the evening, something to tell her friends at the next society meeting she attended back in New York. Still, murder was always a sobering experience.

Pen's eyes slid to the bar, thinking she should perhaps get her cousin some more "medicinal" brandy. Lucien and Honorine were chatting in an awfully familiar manner while sipping the drinks they'd just been handed. There were two people near the top of her list of suspects, at least if one believed Monsieur Padou's revelations. She was even more suspicious when she saw Honorine subtly slip a black and gold lighter to Lucien, the same one Pen had seen him use when she first encountered him in this very lounge. How had Honorine gotten a hold of it?

"Did you see that?"

"See what?" Richard asked.

Pen continued to stare at the two. "I think Honorine and Lucien know each other better than they are letting on."

"Is that so?"

"I'm going to get Cousin a drop of brandy."

"*Penelope.*"

She ignored the warning tone of Richard's voice and

strolled over to the bar. Honorine was the first to notice her, and greeted her with a smile that was almost knowing. It was as if she suspected there would be a bit of interrogating to come.

"Sorry to interrupt," Pen said, returning a smile. She noted the way Lucien casually slipped the lighter into his pocket. "I see you found your lighter?"

"Ah yes, it seems to have been...*discovered* by Madame DuBois," he said, cynically arching one eyebrow at Honorine.

"Did you two meet here on the train?"

There was a pause before Honorine exhaled a tinkling bit of laughter.

Lucien arched a brow again, now directed at Pen. "That sounded like an accusation. I admit Madame has certain charms that appeal to men, however I am in fact a gentleman. I would never take such advantage of a widow."

"I doubt that," Honorine said in a teasing voice. She cast an amused but speculative look toward Penelope. "However, I do believe you are correct, she still suspects us, Monsieur Vollant."

"I'm simply curious as to how you ended up with his lighter. I haven't seen you smoke once on this voyage, nor have you smelled of cigarettes."

"Oh, I don't smoke."

Penelope waited, then realized she was being toyed with. "So you needed it to burn down the train, perhaps."

Honorine laughed again. "No, no, nothing that *diabolique*."

Again, Penelope waited, this time realizing she wouldn't be getting an explanation. Honorine had no reason to reveal anything to her. Even if Penelope thought she was guilty of something, she was not the police, nor had she any power to arrest her. Pen sighed and returned to Richard's side.

"No luck?" he teased.

Pen scowled. "She's definitely hiding something. Perhaps the two of them are conspiring." She turned to see Lucien giving Honorine a nod, then return to the chair across from Cosette. He leaned in to say something to her, yet another remark that she found irritating. Penelope wasn't surprised when she stood up with a determined look on her face.

"I'm exhausted. I would like to go back to my compartment," Cosette threw up her hands. "I have paid for a sleeper car and yet, I am not sleeping."

Simon instantly protested. "I am afraid I cannot—"

However, Cosette was having none of it. "I am not even in the same car as Aristide's body! How can my compartment be a crime scene? You have been so concerned about us being too drunk to speak with the police when we arrive, what if I am too tired? I am liable to fall asleep during any interrogation. How would that look?"

"I'm quite sleepy myself," Margaret pleaded. "Edward and I have had a rather exhausting day."

"My sister has a point. We didn't even know about this blasted Monkey."

Simon, André, and the conductor all seemed ready to argue.

"A solution perhaps," Richard interjected. "It is true that the second car is a crime scene, but the first and third First Class cars are not. Under any other circumstance, residents would be allowed to return to their living quarters. My understanding is that three of the compartments of the third car are empty. Why not allow those who need a rest to occupy those?"

"But there are four of us," Margaret protested.

"Monsieur Padou will remain in our custody right here," Simon said. "Further, we will be holding onto his book as evidence in our investigation."

"You can't—"

"I can. You have already confessed to a conspiracy, even if the Golden Monkey you traded for was a forgery."

"But..." Monsieur Padou looked disheartened, then angry. "I will be making a full accounting of the contents when it is returned to me...with my lawyer present."

Simon seemed unconcerned as he glanced at his partner to make sure he firmly held onto it.

"It is settled, then," Cosette said, walking toward the exit before anyone could protest further. "You can search my room. I don't care. I have nothing to hide."

"Mademoiselle!" Simon shouted after her. He cursed in French, then sent André after her. André placed the book at the end of the bar, then ran after her. The conductor went as well, remembering that Cosette may have been a suspect but she was also a First Class passenger. Simon stayed behind, offering a warning look to everyone, should they decide to leave without permission.

There was the sound of an argument, now in French. Penelope caught only bits of it, but it certainly sounded like Cosette was winning, especially when she heard crying. The woman was an expert on how to manipulate men. She wasn't surprised when a few minutes later the two men returned, looking battle-worn. They conversed with Simon for a moment, a brief argument ensuing, before he finally seemed to relent.

"I think..." Simon began, pausing to give an aggrieved sigh, "it is permissible for those of you in the first and third cars to retire to your compartments. However, no one will be entering their rooms until André has performed a search. If you protest, then you will stay here in the lounge until we reach Lyon. The conductor will follow to arrange quarters for those of you who were in the second car."

"I am not at all tired. How could I be with all of this excitement?" Honorine said with a smile. "I'm perfectly content to lounge on one of the couches here. Mica will keep me company." She gave the bartender a wink.

If her room had not already been searched, Penelope would have automatically considered that a nod toward her guilt. Honorine seemed to be fully aware of that based on the impish smile on her face.

Simon turned to the concierges. "Quentin, you will remain here to help me see to those who choose to remain. Jules, Adrien, if you will return to your respective cars to keep watch over those who wish to retire to their quarters?"

"I think perhaps I shall retire as well," Lucien said, a cryptic smile touching his lips as he eyed everyone in the room. "It has been a most…enlightening voyage."

Margaret and Edward both got up to go to their new rooms in the third car as well. Pen saw Lucien slow down to walk with them. He leaned over and whispered something to Margaret, which had her swiveling her head, giving him an incredulous look. Edward, having overheard, looked perfectly incensed. The brother and sister hurried out ahead of Lucien. All three were escorted by André who held Lucien back a step or two, perhaps to give him a stern talking-to based on the expression on his face.

The conductor consulted Quentin and Simon in private, then turned to the room. "I must return to my duties. You are safe here with Quentin and Monsieur Pougnet. Once again, I apologize for any inconvenience this has all caused. I am sure the company will make adequate compensation for your troubles." With a quick bow, he escaped back to the front of the train.

"Cousin, perhaps you'd like to retire as well?" Penelope offered.

Cousin Cordelia looked at Benny and Lulu, who made it quite evident they wanted to stay, then she straightened a bit and shook her head with a show of nonchalance. "I do feel a bit less tired now."

Benny grinned and patted her hand. "That's right, dove. Besides, you'll be safer here with us."

Lulu pursed her lips across to him, biting back her smile. She then turned to Penelope with a questioning look. "I assume you have some thoughts on all of this."

"Oh, she thinks I am the culprit," Honorine said with one side of her mouth hitched up as she sauntered over. She pulled a chair from one of the tables and brought it closer to the couch where the three of them sat. She took her seat and casually leaned back, taking a sip of her drink as she eyed everyone over the rim.

"I do still wonder what you were doing with Lucien's lighter." Penelope brought her own chair over to join them, sitting across from Honorine. Richard did the same, pulling his chair next to hers.

"There are many reasons a woman might need a lighter," Honorine said in an idle tone. "Perhaps I was lighting a candle? The light may have gone out in my compartment and I needed to see something in the darkness?"

"A man has been murdered, Madame DuBois," Richard reminded her.

"And it is tragic," Honorine said, looking solemn for a brief moment before a speculative look came to her face. "However, it seems he was not the most honorable man. I do wonder how many more people the departed individual may have—what is that funny word you Americans have for it?— *chiseled*? Even beyond those on this train who are working on behalf of his victims?"

"Once a devil, always a devil, and don't I know it," Lulu said.

Penelope thought that rather apt, considering she'd admitted to her romantic involvement with Tommy Callahan, a known gangster. Pen tactfully avoided bringing that up, but she did note Lulu's wry look her way, as though she could read her mind.

"Not all devils are bad, of course," Benny said, waggling his eyebrows. "Wicked perhaps, but hardly evil."

"Whatever does that mean?" Cousin Cordelia asked.

"Never you mind him, honey," Lulu said.

"I firmly agree. I myself have lived quite the wicked life, at least according to my *grand-mère*, rest her soul," Honorine said. "But is it really wicked if it's for the sake of justice?"

"Are you going to tell us what you did with that lighter or not? If it wasn't a cigarette, perhaps you were burning a bit of incriminating evidence?"

"Ah, see now you are using your head, *ma cherie*." Honorine lifted her glass toward Pen.

Penelope blinked in surprise. "Are you testing me?"

"Testing?" Honorine's eyes went wide with feigned ignorance.

"Perhaps it's simply a private matter, Penelope dear," Cousin Cordelia said in a censuring tone.

"I say it was a sordid bit of correspondence. Something daring and wicked between Monsieur Vollant and Madame DuBois."

"Monsieur, you do have the most devilish mind," Honorine said with a sly look toward Benny.

"Or with Mademoiselle Cochet," Lulu offered, giving Benny a conspiratorial grin.

"*Lucille!*" Cousin Cordelia gasped.

Benny, Lulu, and Honorine laughed.

"I do believe we are making our voyeur blush," Honorine said, lifting her glass to Simon who was standing near the bar behind Penelope. From there he could easily hear their conversation.

"No, it wasn't something that illicit," Pen said, narrowing her eyes as she studied Honorine. "It was something you didn't want our *voyeur* to see. I still think it was the telegram you received. Once Monsieur Barbier was found murdered, you knew it might further incriminate you. It was smart to get rid of it, if indeed that is why you stole the lighter. Though, there is one thing that still bothers me about that supposed telegram."

All her friends' eyes were studying Penelope with interest, but none more intently than Honorine's. There was still that hint of amused unconcern, as though she was not at all worried about what Penelope might be about to reveal.

However, before Pen could utter a word, André rushed in with a horrified look on his face. "It is Monsieur Vollant, he has been poisoned!"

CHAPTER TWENTY-FOUR

Simon instantly became alert at André's announcement that Lucien had been poisoned. The shock of it seemed to at first paralyze everyone, then like a popped balloon, they reacted at the same time.

Cousin Cordelia cried out in horror. Lulu and Benny on either side of her cast wide eyes at each other. Richard shot out of his seat, but then thought better of leaving. Penelope exhaled a breath that seemed to take all her air with it.

"Who did it?" Honorine asked, sitting up straighter with a suddenly serious expression on her face.

André was already preoccupied with Simon, who was perfectly incensed. "How could you let this happen?"

"It was poison, someone put it in his glass. How was I to know?" André spat back at his partner.

Simon turned to everyone, but looked at Honorine and Penelope in particular. "All of you are to remain here. Quentin, you are to watch them."

Quentin looked as though his cup had runneth over with responsibilities quite a while back. A look of incomprehension colored his face. Still, he swallowed hard and managed a reluctant nod. Penelope sympathized with him. Two murders on a train were two more than most service workers were used to. At least there was very likely a connection between the two.

Penelope certainly hoped so.

Cousin Cordelia was still in a state. Pen gave Richard a grateful smile when he, without asking, walked over to get a splash more brandy for her. Frankly, Pen could have used another drink herself, but she wanted a clear mind, especially now that it seemed the murderer had no qualms about killing again.

"If it makes you feel better, madame, the two murders are surely connected," Honorine said, giving Cousin Cordelia a reassuring smile. At least she was of the same mind as Penelope.

"It most certainly does not," Pen's cousin argued. "Monsieur Vollant may not have been a gentleman, but that hardly warrants his *murder*."

"Perhaps it was *not* being a gentleman that got him killed," Lulu offered.

"Odd, he certainly seemed the cunning sort. Those scalawags are usually the ones who finish on top," Benny said. He and Lulu cast a conspiratorial look at each other. If any two people were familiar with "scalawags" of all flavors it was them. Then again, Penelope could hardly claim to be so innocent.

"He obviously let his guard down around the wrong person," Richard said thoughtfully. "I'd be curious to know with whom he was at the time of his murder, or more importantly, just prior to it."

"There was—"

"I saw—"

Both Penelope and Honorine had spoken at the same

time. Pen looked her way, and Honorine graciously bowed her head and waved her on to speak first.

"By all means, *mon amie*."

"I was just going to say that I did see him speaking with Edward and Margaret. Neither of them seemed happy about whatever he was saying. I also saw Lucien and Margaret having a heated conversation in private earlier."

"He did seem to hint that he knew more about them than they let on," Richard said.

"He seemed to know quite a bit about almost everyone. For instance, Cosette," Pen turned to give Honorine a pointed look, "and others."

Honorine simply returned a placid smile. "Yes, he did seem awfully...omniscient, no?"

"If Lucien was poisoned, that means it was presumably put into his drink," Pen said.

"Oh my," Cousin Cordelia said, looking down at her own glass with a frown.

"So who was he with from the moment he got his drink, to the moment he...succumbed?" Lulu asked.

Penelope was the first to boldly look Honorine's way. She had been standing right next to him when he was handed the drink, and the two of them had been awfully chummy before parting ways.

"It was not *moi*," Honorine said dryly. "The only thing I gave him was his lighter."

That was a subject to be revisited at some point. Penelope still had that nagging question about these supposed telegrams. For now, she was more concerned about mentally listing everyone who had been close enough to Lucien to poison him.

"He and Cosette have been doing the tango this entire train ride, quite passionately I might add," Benny said. "And an entire car to themselves?" He raised his brow as though he didn't need to go into detail what he was suggesting.

"She is a definite consideration. Of course, we have to include Margaret and Edward." Pen turned to Richard. "As you stated we shouldn't rule anyone out. Adrien, Jules, and André all left with him, the latter even pulling him aside to converse in private."

Richard nodded once in acknowledgment. "And as you pointed out, my dear, the focus should be on who is most plausible as a suspect."

"Of course, darling." She was glad he didn't add his usual caution against playing detective. By now he knew it would fall on deaf ears.

"This is all very charming, but can we return to dabbling into who may have done poor Lucien in?" Benny said in a droll voice.

Penelope rolled her eyes at him, but agreed. "If they are connected, then it would have to be someone who had a window of opportunity to access Monsieur Barbier's compartment to murder him, but also have access to Lucien's drink."

All eyes turned to Honorine, as she fit perfectly within both windows.

"I feel perhaps I should leave," she said cheerily. "It seems I am once again under the, ah, glass device with which to make things easier to view? What is it called?"

"Magnifying glass," Penelope said, though she had the idea Honorine knew perfectly well the correct term.

"Ah yes, magnifying glass. That is a thought, perhaps we should ask the one who has been able to see everything clearly?" She looked past Penelope. "Quentin, *s'il vous plaît?*"

Pen turned to see Quentin look startled at first, then

instantly become professional and join their little grouping. Simon was quietly giving André an earful. From his gesture, she could see him ordering his partner to stay there while he went to the third car to investigate and perhaps gather everyone in the lounge once again.

"How may I be of service, Madame DuBois?" Quentin asked.

"Did you see me enter the second car after bringing Monsieur Barbier's dinner to his room?"

He gently shook his head. "No, Madame. I did not see anyone enter my car after I returned with Monsieur Barbier's dinner, not until dinner service had ended, of course. Monsieur and Madame Smith—" He paused, realizing that wasn't their real name, but then continued. "—they were already there, but left when I arrived."

"I saw her during dinner. She remained in the lounge," Richard said. Honorine gave him a dazzling smile.

Penelope pursed her lips, then turned her attention back to Quentin. "But you *did* leave with Officer Pougnet and Officer Robineau for a period of time toward the end of dinner. Were you back at your station when Madame DuBois returned to her compartment?" She knew the answer, as he had still been gone when she and Richard passed through his carriage to get to the first one.

He swallowed and cast a quick, uncomfortable glance to Honorine. She nodded as though giving him permission to answer the question. "No. In fact, I did not see anyone return to their room. Again, I did alert both Adrien and Jules so that service would be minimally affected."

"Of course," Penelope said, then gave him an apologetic look. "It must be difficult, having to remain so professional under the circumstances. I'm sure you were not expecting a murder to happen in your car."

"No, mademoiselle, it is not something I have experienced before."

"I should hope *not*," Cousin Cordelia said.

"Merci, Quentin," Honorine said, relieving the poor man, who happily moved further away. Honorine turned back to the rest of them, her lower lip plumped out. "Alors, I realize this does nothing to prove my innocence. If you are concerned I may murder any of you, I am happy to return to the bar. Mica is such good company. I am sure there is another bottle of champagne for him to open for me."

Cousin Cordelia was the only one who seemed to take her seriously, looking at her as though she had just confessed to murder.

"But it would be so dull without you, dove," Benny said with a pout.

Lulu offered a sly smile. "As long as I remain alive, I have no objections."

"Lucille," Cousin Cordelia admonished.

If anyone was inclined to protest, far more distracting fare overshadowed their complaints. The first of the other passengers who had been in the third car when Lucien was poisoned entered the lounge.

CHAPTER TWENTY-FIVE

Everyone could hear Cosette before she even entered the car. Her protests in French were impossible to ignore. All heads in the lounge turned as Simon manhandled her through the door.

"My, I wonder who they suspect did poor Lucien in," Benny muttered in a sarcastic voice as he watched Simon practically toss Cosette into a chair.

"It was not me," Cosette spat, glaring at Simon. "Why would I be stupid enough to kill him while he was in my compartment? Someone obviously put the poison into his drink before our meeting."

Penelope wanted to sympathize, but this was the same woman who had accused her friend. Besides, there were only so many suspects and Cosette certainly seemed to have a thorny relationship with Lucien. They were also both after the Golden Monkey, so why not eliminate the competition? Resentment and greed made for two very compelling motives. Now, it seemed Lucien had been in her compartment when he died?

Margaret and Edward entered the car next. The former

looked pale and stricken. Her brother seemed defensive as ever, as though waiting to argue with anyone who might accuse him of anything. Adrien and Jules followed, both understandably looking battle-worn.

Penelope revisited the discussion their little group had just vacated in favor of the return of their fellow passengers. If Honorine was a likely suspect, so were they. Edward and Margaret had exited with Lucien, close enough to have put something into his drink. Their relationship with him certainly wasn't amicable. If anything, they seemed more resentful of him than even Cosette. Like her, they had something they wanted from Aristide.

"It was not me, I did not kill Lucien....or Aristide," Cosette continued.

"You were very quick to condemn others when Monsieur Barbier's body was found," Penelope pointed out. She was still angry about her friend being accused of murder.

Her gaze faltered, and Penelope was surprised to see a look of regret come to her face. It seemed genuine. She turned to Lulu and then Honorine. "I am sorry for having accused both of you before. I was...I was distraught, in shock from the murder."

"That is easy enough to say now," Penelope said, not so easily swayed.

"I accept your apology." Honorine gave Cosette a speculative look. "However, I would like to know more. You said you met Monsieur Barbier while in Menton?"

Cosette narrowed her eyes as though wondering if there was a trap in Honorine's question.

"That's what she said," Lulu answered, her voice not quite as sympathetic as Honorine's.

Cosette looked briefly irritated, then chagrined as she

met Lulu's gaze. "I have apologized, mademoiselle. I truly am sorry," she said, sounding believably contrite. "Of course I don't believe you killed Aristide."

Lulu must have sensed how sorry she truly was and replied in a slightly more sympathetic tone. "You aren't helping yourself by keeping quiet, honey."

Cosette shook her head and lowered her gaze. "I did not kill Aristide or Lucien, that is all I can say."

Honorine continued, undeterred as she seemed to wonder aloud. "It is odd that you were so close to Monsieur Barbier, yet you did not realize he was bringing the Golden Monkey of Kashmir on board this train to make a trade? Nor did you know about the ticket he purchased for the second compartment. Considering the only reason you were with him was because of this Golden Monkey, it does make you seem rather....*délinquante*."

Cosette seemed both indignant and even more suspicious. She wasn't the only one. Penelope wondered what Honorine was after. This was something more than insulting her as some form of revenge. From the curious expressions of everyone else, they felt the same.

"What is your point, madame?" Cosette asked tersely.

"Was it really the Golden Monkey you were after?" Honorine sounded surprisingly sympathetic in her tone, rather than accusatory. Now, Penelope was even more curious.

Cosette seemed ready to give a sharp retort, then thought better of it. Instead, she turned her head, completely silent as to any further questions.

Penelope sighed in frustration. Honorine had done nothing but prevent any further conversation with her odd questions. Still, she figured it wouldn't hurt to ask a few of her own. The worst that could happen was that Cosette would continue to remain silent.

"Can you tell us what Lucien was doing in your compartment?" Pen asked, then realized how the question could be interpreted, and quickly added, "Perhaps you two were discussing the Golden Monkey of Kashmir?"

Cosette offered Pen a dry look. "Yes, we were talking, that is all."

At least it was an answer. Pen briefly wondered why she was so willing to discuss the more touchy subjects of the murders or Lucien as opposed to her relationship with Monsieur Barbier. However, she wasn't about to pause long enough to ponder it while she still had Cosette talking. "I assume the two of you decided to meet via the connecting doors? Or perhaps Adrien saw him enter your compartment through the outer door?"

Cosette was smart enough to realize Adrien, standing right there in the lounge, could confirm one way or the other, and her expression became even more sardonic. "Yes, through our connecting doors."

Which meant she would have had to unlock and open her own to a man she so outwardly seemed to despise. Pen decided to push further. "I suppose it is fortuitous that your compartment happened to open to his. Odd that Monsieur Barbier would have agreed to such an arrangement."

"*Penelope*," Cousin Cordelia said, scandalized.

Pen kept her attention on Cosette, whose expression now held nothing but contempt. "Non, madame, it is fine. I am used to such insulting accusations. I cannot explain the arrangement. Nor can Aristide, as *someone* in this room killed him. That someone is not *moi!*"

"That remains to be seen. When we reach Lyon you will be formally placed under arrest, Mademoiselle

Cochet," Simon interjected, having heard that outburst. "I should warn you, anything said presently may be used as part of that investigation and during your trial. However, if you have anything to say about the missing Golden Monkey," he cast a brief, scrutinizing glance toward Monsieur Padou, "fake or otherwise, that may help prove your innocence, I would be very curious to hear it."

Cosette glared at him. She was smart enough to stop talking at that point, and deliberately turned away to face the window.

It was all very strange. Cosette was quite obviously hiding something, but what was it? Honorine seemed to be hinting at it. Did she already know, or was she simply fishing? There seemed to be more to Cosette's adventure with the murdered Aristide Barbier than a simple procurement of a stolen artifact. Anyone else would be frantically voicing their defense, that they had only cozied up to him to obtain the Golden Monkey. Cosette was only making herself look suspicious.

On the other hand, there was a brother and sister who not only had every reason to want Aristide dead, but they had a very nice window of opportunity during dinner. Penelope turned to find Edward and Margaret huddled together, both looking quite anxious.

CHAPTER TWENTY-SIX

Edward was the first to notice Penelope staring at him just a bit too long and he glared at her. Margaret followed his gaze, and her eyes widened with alarm.

"If you plan on accusing us again, this time for Lucien's murder, get it over with," Edward spat. "We've already told you our secrets, which most certainly don't include murder."

"So you claim," Penelope said. "There was still the opportunity to later kill Monsieur Barbier when Quentin was with the officers."

"Oh for heaven's sake!" Margaret erupted. "You seem intent on laying blame on everyone. We've told you he was in his room and very much alive when we left at dinner. Quentin all but confirmed he still was when we left. When we returned after dinner, we were in our own rooms. It's bad enough that we will likely never retrieve mother's money, but now we may end up being arrested for a crime we didn't commit?"

"Me thinks the lady doth protest too much," Benny muttered under his breath, but not quietly enough.

"Oh, do shut up!" Margaret spat, getting even more hysterical.

Though she was sympathetic to their plight, Penelope wasn't cowed quite so easily. "What is it Lucien said to you just prior to your return to your compartments? He whispered something to you, what was it?"

Rather than answer, Margaret's face colored. Filled with outrage, she spun to Simon and André. "Are you going to allow this? She's taking over your case! She's not an officer of the law."

Simon placed a restraining hand on André before he could speak first. "No, she is not. However, we cannot prevent a woman from posing questions. Just as we cannot prevent you from answering in a manner that you see fit. You are perfectly at liberty to defend yourself, mademoiselle."

Penelope almost admired that bit of manipulation. Of course the police would not interfere with a member of the public doing their work for them, unrestrained by the bounds of regulations and proper procedure. They would be even more appreciative if suspects blabbed about their misdeeds or anything that could be used against them in court. No wonder they had allowed Penelope, and Honorine for that matter, to play the amateur detectives for so long.

"Lucien was simply taunting us," Edward said. "The man was a pest who was only interested in stirring up trouble. Certainly nothing worth killing over. How would we have even come across any poison that might have killed him? Do you presume we simply travel around France with it in our luggage?"

"One might think you had reason to kill *another* person

on board, if not Lucien," Honorine said. "One who just happens to be dead."

"One might presume the same of you," Margaret retorted.

"And for what reason? Because a client was wronged? By the time of his death, I had already discovered the means to procure justice on her behalf. If I murdered every odious man a client had been injured by, half the men in France would be dead. And really, these women would be far more likely to do the deed themselves."

"Perhaps if you simply repeated what he told you it would solve the matter of suspicion," Penelope offered.

Edward lifted his chin with haughty indignation. Margaret seemed filled with disgust, but she was the one to finally answer. "There was some *allusion* to...incestuous relations. That the British, the English in particular, were well known for turning their noses up at anyone who wasn't decidedly English, and that perhaps Edward and I had taken that notion to an extreme."

Cousin Cordelia gasped in scandalized surprise. Benny snorted out a laugh, which only had the siblings going red. Honorine wasn't quite so restrained, her lyrical laugh filling the air. Lulu hummed in a tone that was somehow both scolding of the unfortunate remarks while also hinting at a bit of amusement as well. Even Monsieur Padou silently shook with laughter. Richard, naturally, maintained a straight face. Simon had a dry smile. André just looked disappointed that it wasn't something more damning. Pen was equally disappointed. It was insulting, certainly, and in a moment of extreme anger, it might have been enough for Edward, at least, to lash out at Lucien. However, poison was the very definition of premeditation. Why poison Lucien over what amounted to nothing more than a schoolboy taunt?

"I'm glad you all find it so amusing," Edward spat, looking even more indignant. "The man obviously said the wrong thing to the wrong person and it got him killed. While I didn't do it myself, nor did my sister, I can't say I don't blame the individual."

"That's as much a confession as anything," André grumbled.

"Oh monsieur, it is not," Honorine countered, her face still grinning with mirth over the puerile insult.

"The fact remains, someone in this room poisoned and killed Monsieur Vollant," Richard said, the serious expression on his face cutting through the amusement of the moment.

That was enough to make everyone somber again. At least until they were shocked into a more overriding emotion upon seeing Lucien himself stumble into the car, looking very green at the gills, but decidedly alive.

"I'm afraid the news of my death has been greatly overstated."

CHAPTER TWENTY-SEVEN

"Mon dieu!" Cosette shot up from her chair, her hand to her mouth in shock at Lucien who, contrary to the most recent news, was in fact alive.

Margaret practically leaped into her brother's arms, like a child who had just been surprised by a spider. For his part, Edward went white as a ghost.

Monsieur Padou simply raised his brow, as though this was nothing more than another small excursion on the eccentricity of the voyage.

There was a smattering of gasps and brief exclamations from Penelope's friends, even Richard, who exhaled a sharp breath.

"Did anyone think to actually make sure Monsieur Vollant was dead?" Honorine asked in a droll voice, quite unnecessarily.

Simon turned to his partner with angry accusation written all over his face. "You did not check to make sure?"

"You were there as well. Did you not check?" André spat back.

"I was relying on you doing your job! How can I trust a partner who does not know a dead man when he sees one?"

André's face darkened, and Penelope was sure he was going to strike his partner. Instead, he quite surprisingly looked, abashed. "I—I..." he turned to give an angry look to Cosette. "She was the one to scream." He turned to Adrien, even angrier. "And you said he was dead."

Adrien looked for all the world as though he wished he had never taken this job. He was older than his fellow concierges, but now seemed to age another ten years. "I was simply assuming. He looked quite dead, monsieur."

"He was, I was sure of it!" Cosette exclaimed.

"Quite obviously not," Lucien said in a dry tone, teetering as he made his way to the bar. "Though someone did try their best." He flashed a sardonic smile, that seemed rather macabre settled amid the pallor and sickly look on his face. He turned to Mica behind the bar, who shied away from him, as though he really was a ghost. *"A water, if you please."*

Simon was still laying into his partner. "How could you not perform the most basic—?"

"Don't be too hard on him," Lucien interjected with a weak smile. "I most likely was dead for a brief period. But alas, God had other plans for me."

"Or perhaps the Devil," Benny said under his breath. Pen saw Lulu reach behind Cousin Cordelia to slap him on the arm.

"At the very least you can tell everyone that it was neither Margaret nor I who poisoned you."

Lucien arched a brow. "I'm afraid I cannot, *mon ami*. I have no idea who poisoned me. Perhaps the same individual who killed Monsieur Barbier?"

"It seems they weren't quite as successful in your case," Penelope said. "How fortuitous for you."

Lucien laughed, though weakly. The effort seemed to cause him pain and he reeled a bit. "Perhaps a certain individual simply wanted to get my attention?" He winked at Cosette. That was enough to have her sitting down, an exhale of irritation escaping her lips.

"That seems rather an extreme measure, no?"

Lucien gave Pen an exaggeratedly wounded look. "Why would anyone want to kill me? I'm a perfect gentleman." A grin curled his lips just before he took a long, grateful sip of the water Mica handed to him.

"Well, you certainly managed to get back into Cosette's good graces. It seems you were with her when you succumbed to this poisoning attempt?"

Even though she couldn't directly see Cosette, Penelope still sensed her attention snapping back to her.

"Ah yes, our *petit rendezvous.*" Lucien's lupine grin came back as he waggled his eyebrows at Cosette sitting behind Pen.

"I have already stated it was a simple conversation," Cosette insisted.

Honorine chimed in. "The topic of which, you have been unwilling to reveal. Perhaps Lucien will be more forthcoming?"

Lucien clucked his tongue. "As I stated, I am a gentleman."

"A gentleman who may be arrested as part of a conspiracy if you don't speak," Simon said. "This poisoning has all been very suspicious."

Lucien shot him an indignant look, then sighed and spoke. "We were discussing the possibility of where the real

Golden Monkey of Kashmir might be, and how to find it. Perhaps split the proceeds."

"And did you come to any conclusions?" Simon asked, a sardonic look on his face.

"Sadly...*non*."

Penelope pursed her lips with annoyance. What a silly thing to be so secretive about. At that point, anyone in First Class who wasn't wondering where the real Golden Monkey was would have to be a saint. Frankly, it made sense that Lucien and Cosette, two individuals practiced in the art of acquiring stolen goods might put aside their differences and join forces. Perhaps they had been working together all along?

Penelope considered that. It was awfully convenient that they had adjoining rooms, but was it too convenient? When factored with all the other discoveries, perhaps it *was* just a coincidence. Lucien had stolen his tickets from a family, one that Penelope had seen looking distraught on her way to board the train. Even if he had somehow known which compartment Cosette would be in—not an impossible idea, if she knew ahead of time and could alert him—he would have had to espy which passengers also had tickets for that particular car and then robbed them of said tickets. That would have been quite a bit of coordination.

The other prickly problem was that of the assigned compartments in that third car. Aristide was in 303, or at least had a ticket for that compartment, while Cosette was in 304. Thus, either he had bought the tickets before the family did, with the intent that he wouldn't have a shared door with Cosette, or the family had bought the tickets first, with the intent that they would be separated. While it made sense that the boy might have his own compartment, he and his sisters were all still young enough that the parents might not have liked having two strangers dividing the family, even if they were in the same car. Further, Aristide had bought his tickets far enough in advance that several parties on board had not only discovered his traveling plans, but also been able to acquire tickets of their own, thanks to whoever had sent Honorine, Edward, and Margaret the helpful telegrams. Thus, it seemed Aristide had deliberately given himself a room that didn't adjoin with his companion. Once again, Penelope had to ask why.

That brought up yet another prickly problem. Surely Aristide would have realized his deceit, switching the real Golden Monkey for the fake, would be discovered while the train was still on its voyage. As Pierre had pointed out, it wasn't as though he could simply flee into the night and disappear with the real Golden Monkey.

"Did you see Monsieur Barbier leave his compartment at all, Quentin, even if only for a moment?" Penelope asked.

"*Non*, mademoiselle. Of course, he could have left while I was procuring his meal."

Penelope turned to Edward and Margaret. Before she could ask, Edward answered her question. "We've already told you, he was in his compartment, holding the door closed, so we could not enter."

"And you were leaving by the time Quentin returned," she pondered. "That does leave a small window of time, before you arrived and after Quentin left. He could have entered the third car to go to his other room at that point."

All eyes turned to Adrien, who blinked in surprise at the sudden onset of attention. He stood straighter, presenting a more dignified figure, and shook his head. "I did not see him enter the third car to go to his room during the meal service, or after. However...I cannot say I didn't *briefly* step away from my post at some point."

"Are you suggesting the Golden Monkey has been in compartment 303 this entire time?" Cosette looked perfectly stunned and not just a tad annoyed.

"It is a possibility. After all, only one Golden Monkey was found in the suitcase taken off the train. I think, after presenting the real one to Monsieur Padou, he may have stayed in his compartment, all for the purpose of switching it out for the fake one, in the hopes Monsieur Padou would not notice. Perhaps that is why he insisted on not being disturbed by Quentin when he returned with his tray. He could have taken advantage of his absence and absconded with it to his second compartment in 303, coincidentally while Adrien had briefly stepped away."

"Did either of you search compartment 303?" Richard asked Simon and André.

The two international police glanced uncomfortably at one another.

"You haven't?" Richard asked, incredulous. Even Penelope was surprised. Granted, it seemed as though Monsieur Barbier had abandoned his original compartment in favor of the second, where his body was found. Further, until they learned there were two Golden Monkeys, and one of them was presumably still on board, they had little reason to search that compartment. Then, of course, Lucien's presumed murder had distracted everyone.

"I will go," Simon said through clenched teeth.

"Are we forgetting something?" Honorine said before he could leave. Simon stopped and turned to frown at her. She darted her eyes to Lucien, sitting on one of the stools near the bar. "You should search the compartment of anyone who had unsupervised access to 303 as well."

All eyes followed hers to Lucien. Honorine had made a good point, one Penelope was certain she would have thought of...eventually. Lucien, presumed dead, had been allowed quite a bit of time without any witnesses present. It had been long enough that he could have easily searched Aristide's second compartment at his leisure. Even Adrien, the concierge for the third car had been brought into the lounge car.

Lucien exhaled an overly aggrieved sigh, then shrugged and waved a hand in the air. "You will find no Golden Monkey in my compartment. I'm beginning to wonder if there really is a second one anywhere on board at all." He cast a speculative look toward Pierre.

Penelope frowned, and she noted Honorine do the same. Neither of them had expected him to be so accommodating. Then, Pen thought better of it. Lucien was a cunning individual, and a fox knew how to avoid being outfoxed. Surely he would have realized that eventually everyone's belongings and compartments would be searched and he would have been a fool to keep the Golden Monkey hidden among his own things.

"I will perform the search," Simon said, giving Lucien an uncertain glance, as though he didn't trust his word either. He also seemed surprised Lucien was so willing to have his room searched. "This *will* include your compartment as well, Monsieur Vollant."

Lucien simply offered a mild, wry smile and lowered his lids in acquiescence.

"I have nothing to hide either," Cosette announced. When everyone turned to her, she glared. "Do not pretend you don't suspect me of something as well."

"How could we? We don't even know your real name," Margaret spat back. "Edward and I have at least revealed who we are."

Cosette's defiant expression faltered for a bit at that

attack. She seemed to have an internal debate, and must have surely realized by now that the police would investigate her once they reached Lyon or at least Paris. There was no longer any point in withholding that information, as it only made her look guilty. She inhaled and sat up straighter before speaking. "Francine Deschamps, that is my real name. I often use an alias in my work. It is no crime."

Lucien laughed, the color coming back into his cheeks. "Now you see why she has chosen Cosette Cochet."

Cosette, or rather, Francine chose to ignore that, her eyes focused on Simon and André. "I no longer have anything to hide. However, it seems the two members of the international police have been quite negligent. A dead man. A fake artifact. One, quite possibly the real one, is still missing. A mistake in declaring a man dead. How are we to feel secure under your incompetence? Or perhaps those mistakes were by design?"

"What are you accusing us of, Mademoiselle?" André looked angry enough to storm over and arrest her on the spot.

Simon placed a restraining hand on his arm, but gave Francine a sardonic look. "Perhaps mademoiselle, who is still very much under suspicion, would like to accompany us during our search?"

Jules stepped forward. "One of us could accompany you, perhaps? Or even the conductor? We are not suspects, are we?"

"Everyone is a suspect, I'm afraid," Simon said.

"Surely you don't suspect a fellow officer of the law?" Penelope said, glancing at Richard. "Why not take Detective Prescott of the New York Police Department with you? He's hardly at the top of your list of suspects."

"*Bien*, Monsieur Prescott will you join me?" Simon gave

a hard, patronizing look to everyone in the room. "Just to reassure everyone."

"Of course," Richard said, standing up.

Penelope took his arm and encouraged him to lean in closer so she could whisper. "If Lucien did take it, he wouldn't be stupid enough to leave it in his room. I would search any of the common areas in the nearby vicinity as well."

He nodded and she let go so he could leave with Simon. However, they were temporarily delayed.

"I think we are missing the most obvious solution to all of this," Honorine announced in an oddly cheerful tone, capturing the attention of everyone, including Richard and Simon, who both stopped to look at her. "Mademoiselle Banks was correct in that this missing Golden Monkey is the key to everything, and we have the answer standing right here in this car, *non*?"

"What would that be?" Penelope asked, truly curious.

"Who sent the telegrams?"

CHAPTER TWENTY-EIGHT

Penelope was the first to address Honorine's statement. "You believe the person who sent the telegrams to the three of you is on this train?"

"*Bien sûr*! It only makes sense, does it not?"

At the very least, Penelope was glad Honorine had decided to revisit that subject. The nagging concern that she had momentarily dismissed after the news of Lucien's poisoning—yet another thing to revisit—was now a priority.

"Do you happen to have your telegram with you?" Penelope asked.

Honorine gave her a conspiratorial smile, as though she knew Pen would ask that very question. "Sadly, I do not. You were right, ma cherie, I did use Monsieur Vollant's lighter to burn it."

"So that's how you 'found' it?" Lucien said, giving her a cool smile, which was almost admiring. "It seems Monsieur Barbier and I have something else in common. We have both been victims of the Widow DuBois...perhaps twice?"

"Only in the return of property," Honorine said, her

eyes wide with innocence. "I am afraid the murder—*attempted* in your case—was not my doing."

"Now, now, cherie, let us not begin telling untruths. You may not be the murderer, but I have been borrowing matches from Mica since dinner, when you just happened to pass me in the lounge. You are quite good, cherie, I did not notice a thing. I'm sure your skill has served you quite well in your profession."

Honorine twisted her lips into a smile, then cast a sly look at Penelope. "He fancies himself quite omniscient, no? I'm afraid I will have to disavow him of that bit of arrogance. I did not steal your lighter, monsieur. I found it."

No one believed that, particularly after she had already confessed to lifting Monsieur Barbier's wallet. However, neither Penelope nor Lucien was interested in arguing the point, as he had his lighter safely back in his pocket.

"Speaking of omniscient, are we supposed to fathom what it was you were about to reveal when we were so rudely interrupted?" Benny asked Penelope. " It had to do with this telegram business."

"I just found it odd that the telegram Edward and Margaret received correctly sent them to Menton, just in time for them to get tickets onboard the train. Why would yours direct you to Monte Carlo?"

Honorine shrugged. "I suppose you would have to ask the individual who sent the telegram."

"I thought we were done with lies."

"What is it you think I am lying about?"

"I don't think you received a telegram at all. I wouldn't be surprised if you were the one who sent the telegram to Edward and Margaret."

Honorine pressed a hand to her chest and offered an overt look of humility. "I am pleased you are so generous in your thoughts." She sighed and removed her hand. "Au contraire, I am afraid, there was indeed a telegram. Quite informative, in fact. I felt bad for my client, as it saved me from having to do much work at all. Though, I confess, I had only just been hired."

"What information did it give you?"

Honorine considered Penelope for only a moment, then shrugged as though there was no longer any reason to withhold the information. "It told me the whereabouts of Monsieur Barbier's money, or that which he had hidden from his wife, particularly which bank and account number under which I could find it. That is why I, ah, *liberated* him of his wallet, only briefly, *bien sûr*. As it happens, my little mouse was quite correct about everything."

"They knew his bank account number?" Richard asked in surprise.

"Indeed."

"That money belongs to our mother!" Margaret said, outraged.

"At least some of it," Edward said, staring at Honorine as though she had been the one to take it.

"I can see why you might want to burn it," Pen said, arching a brow. "It's quite damning."

"Perhaps even illegal," Simon offered, though without much threat behind it. He and André seemed more curious than suspicious.

"It seems your little mouse didn't give you all the right information," Lulu pointed out. "Why send you to Monte Carlo instead of Menton?"

Honorine seemed to ponder it only for a moment. "Perhaps because my client was less sympathetic? Yes, Madame Barbier was terribly wronged by her husband, but she was not left completely impoverished. She is still very well set. I believe it was anger more than anything that fueled her desire to find him. However...." She cast a look toward Edward and Margaret.

Penelope was the one to ask. "What did your telegram say?"

Edward and Margaret cast a quick, furtive look toward one another, both reluctant to reveal anything.

"It is quite obvious, no?" Honorine finally said. "They also had the same information about bank accounts."

Edward snapped his attention to her, angry that she had answered for them. The guilty look on Margaret's face told Pen that Honorine had spoken the truth. Which begged the question...

"How would you know that?"

Honorine threw her hands up and exhaled an exasperated sigh. "Because of course it would! Why would theirs be any different? Why give me more information to access the money, but delay my access to Monsieur Barbier? Then to give them his correct location only to leave them without any information on how to get their money? It makes no sense. *Non, amie,* someone has been playing the Good Samaritan in order of need it seems."

"And you believe that someone is on this train?" André asked.

Honorine arched an eyebrow his way. "I do."

"It does make sense," Benny mused. "If I had created such chaos, I would like to see the fruits of my labor as it played out."

"Of course you would," Lulu said, giving him a sardonic smile. "But I agree. It does make sense. This individual obviously meant for one of you to act on the information. Perhaps they had even planned on adding a bit of...encouragement if needed."

"Except a murder intervened," Richard said.

"Which makes it unlikely this person is also the murderer," Honorine offered.

"Not necessarily," Pen countered. "The murder weapon was Monsieur Barbier's own letter opener. It had his initials on it. It could still be a crime of passion that our Good Samaritan took advantage of in the moment. It's all the more likely if they were close enough to him, or had investigated him enough—" She gave Honorine a pointed look. "— to know so much about him."

Honorine leaned forward and a studious expression came to her face. "Oui, oui, that is an interesting point. As Mademoiselle Banks correctly assumes, I, as a private investigator, am likely to have discovered so much information about Monsieur Barbier. However, if you question my client, his wife, she will confirm that I was only recently hired. I am quite good at what I do, *hélas*, I am not that good."

"*Simplement* very good at stealing," Lucien muttered.

"*Oui*, it can be a very valuable tool. I would happily teach you?"

"Do you have any proof of who this person might be?" André interjected.

"I do have thoughts," Honorine said, giving him a frank look.

"She suspects one of you," Penelope said, eager to get back on topic as well.

Simon breathed out an incredulous laugh. André simply exhaled with impatience, as though she was wasting their time.

"Why would we do such a thing?" Simon asked.

"That is the question that we should be asking," Penelope answered. "There are two parts to this. One, someone who has spent time learning as much as they can about Monsieur Barbier. Two, and more importantly, someone who had a reason to do such a thing. Does it not make sense that it would be one of you? You'd have a number of resources at your disposal to not only investigate him, but do it legally."

"That can be a hindrance more than an asset," Richard pointed out. "Yes, you would be able to question and investigate under the authority of the law, which does instill a bit more cooperation, but you are also bound by acting within the scope of what is allowed within proper procedure."

"I think it is already established by the very nature of the telegrams being sent, this individual," she turned to Simon and André, "or individuals are not too concerned about proper legal procedure. I doubt the Commission would look fondly upon such an act, as benevolent as it was."

"Exactly. Why would we risk our careers doing such a thing?" André said.

"Why would someone risk their freedom by committing murder?" Honorine said with a shrug.

"Motivation can be a powerful force," Penelope added. "But I think we are ignoring an alternate perspective. Yes, an officer of the law would have certain benefits, as would someone with whom Monsieur Barbier would willingly cooperate." She turned to Pierre. "Monsieur Padou could have demanded certain access before agreeing to a purchase. An eager seller would agree to certain terms. However," she said, looking around the room. "There is someone who had even more, shall we say, intimate access to him."

Most everyone fully understood that reference and every eye turned to Francine. She had already taken on a defensive stance, her chin lifted and eyes narrowed. "I do not know what you are talking about."

"Every woman knows how to use her innate abilities to charm a man," Penelope said, sympathetically. "And you are quite beautiful. It has no doubt been quite beneficial in your chosen profession."

"The profession in which I am only after the Golden Monkey of Kashmir."

"And yet, you were not even aware Monsieur Barbier had brought it on board? Two of them in fact! I am sorry, but, you must be quite inept at your chosen profession to have secured a train ticket to join him, but be completely unaware he was transporting the very thing you have been after, which would fetch you quite a fortune."

"*Exactement!*" Francine said. "So, why would I risk it for these people who have no gratitude?" She glared at Edward and Margaret, then turned her venom on Honorine. "And a woman who would nearly throw it all away by stealing his wallet?"

Benny chuckled. "Again, me thinks—"

"—the woman doth protest too much," Penelope finished for him. "Or perhaps she doth protest in a very suspicious way."

"What do you mean?"

"To be quite frank, Mademoiselle Cochet—or should I say Mademoiselle Deschamps—your protest sounds more like one of frustration than defense or indignation. Like a parent who has given their child all the means to succeed, and yet they fail."

"I beg your pardon?" Edward protested. "What exactly were we to do with a telegram from an anonymous source that claims to know where our mother's money is?"

"*Pour l'amour du Ciel!*" Mademoiselle Deschamps exclaimed. "You were to get the money for your mother!"

Penelope sat up straighter in surprise. She wasn't the only one. While everyone physically reacted in a similar manner, none emitting anything more than a small gasp, Francine filled the silence with her French curses.

"*Mon dieu!*" She shot up from her chair and began pacing. "*It was practically handed to you on a silver platter. All you had to do was get the money. The train was meant to be a last resort, you could confront him, have him arrested at least!*"

"Francine," Lucien uttered, hoping to capture her attention. All hints of that rakish charm were gone now, replaced by something that radiated sympathy. "*That is enough.*"

"*But it is not!* Don't you see?"

"What I see is a woman who seems to have had a grudge against Monsieur Barbier," Simon announced. "A woman, who could have just as easily murdered Monsieur Barbier when her plan did not work. So, perhaps you should explain why you were so eager to help Monsieur Barbier's enemies, *Madame Deschamps?*"

CHAPTER TWENTY-NINE

Cosette, now going by her real name of Francine, stopped her pacing and stared at Simon as though suddenly realizing she was not in the lounge car alone. That in fact, everyone from First Class was there with her...and they were still reeling from the revelation that she had been the one to send the telegrams to Edward, Margaret, and Honorine.

"Again, Mademoiselle Deschamps, why did you send these telegrams?" Simon asked, this time more sympathetic than accusatory. Perhaps he was hoping that would disarm her enough to get her talking, or perhaps he empathized with whatever her motives were. Either way, it worked.

"I..." she walked back to her chair and sagged into it. "Like the Stillmans, my mother had been targeted by Monsieur Barbier. Sadly, she is no longer alive to benefit from my having finally found him. My father had died and left us only a small sum. My mother had been frail even before that. What Aristide did, she never recovered from." She arched a brow as her gaze filled with venom. "That seems to have been Aristide's favorite target. Women in such situations are quite vulnerable, desperate even. More importantly, they are often ignorant when it comes to matters of finance. I was only sixteen at the time, and Paris was no place where someone so young as myself or as sickly as my mother could find adequate work. The war had turned everyone into vultures."

She looked out the window, a cynical, humorous smile on her face before she turned back to them, all hints of amusement gone. "Of course a pretty, young woman never has to suffer for long. She learns how to use her charms—at first, simply to get a warm meal. It would have been easy to sell my soul—and, of course, something else—but my mother was still alive at the time. She would have seen it in my eyes, and I could not do that to her. It would have been the thing that finally killed her. I am not sorry to say, that did lead me down a far more mercenary path. I felt no guilt when it came to taking advantage of wealthy men. The way they were with me, as though I was nothing more than a pretty statue or adornment in the room, they deserved it. They couldn't fathom that I had any intelligence or cunning." She laughed. "Their office desks remained unlocked. Their meetings with partners and financial advisors were held behind doors that weren't even fully closed."

"Francine," Lucien said softly, his eyes sliding to Simon and André.

"What do they matter? If any man wanted to file a complaint or charge against me, they would have by now. Their pride would never allow it. I welcome facing them in court, watching the public humiliation they would be exposed to." A bitter smile came to her face. "But no...that would never happen."

There was another pause as she turned to stare out the window. This time it was a bit longer before she spoke again. "When my mother finally succumbed to her illness, her final bit of advice to me was to use my skills to a better end, one that was less likely to have me facing prison. There were far more deserving targets for everything I had learned. Simply being wealthy was not a sin." Her gaze traveled to Lucien and a small smile came to her lips. "That's when I found a teacher, one who was almost as unscrupulous as I once was."

"Oh I still very much am, cherie," Lucien said with a devilish grin, but there was a tiny spark of affection in his eyes. "That is why I followed you onto this train."

Francine glared at him. "You nearly ruined everything. A scorpion never changes."

"He's worse than a scorpion," Margaret accused. She turned to Simon and André. "He tried to blackmail me earlier. He said he knew Edward and I weren't a newly married couple, that we were hiding something. That he wouldn't reveal our secret if we paid him."

"He was quite obviously fishing, Margaret. I told you that. He knew you'd be the one to let the secret slip and you did. If it hadn't been for the murder, forcing our hand, he might have gotten away with it." Edward glared at Lucien, who simply returned an insolent shrug.

So that was what Penelope had witnessed when she first entered the lounge earlier. Lucien really was the predatory sort. Of course, the matter was quite moot by then, and the looks of indifference on everyone's face revealed as much. Simon was concerned with the more pressing issue of Francine's revelation.

"So you have been working with Mademoiselle

Deschamps this entire time?" Simon demanded, his voice filled with outrage as he stared at Lucien.

Lucien's brow rose and he grinned. "*Au contraire, mon ami*, I am here for the Golden Monkey of Kashmir. I wanted it all for myself. How could I ignore such a prize? As Mademoiselle Deschamps has stated, I am thoroughly unscrupulous."

"So you sent the telegrams because you no longer needed to recover the money for your mother?" Penelope asked Francine.

"I had been searching for him for years, learning only of a man who had done the same to others, as Monsieur Padou has claimed. I first had to learn his real name. Then, finally, after so long, I learned through various illegitimate sources that a certain artifact was for sale to the right buyer. There was a description, even the name he used when he preyed upon my mother." A wry smile came to her face. "It was him. But yes, I had no need of the money for myself. However, I was certain I was not the only one he had wronged. At the time, I learned through my sources, that one private investigator and two siblings were also in search of the same man. Why not allow them to accomplish what I could not?

"All I knew was that he was in Menton. It did not take long to find him. Aristide likes the finer things, this includes his preference for women. I made myself seem...expensive, unattainable. He was like a kitten to cream, and just as unsuspecting." She smiled, pleased with herself. She turned to Honorine. "Yes, I did give the others an advantage. Madame Barbier is still a wealthy woman. However, I am aware of your reputation Madame DuBois. I knew you would succeed in finding him, accessing the money, and ruining him. I am also aware of Madame Barbier's reputation for being ruthless."

"It seems someone has been even more ruthless," Honorine said, with one brow arched.

"So, you knew about the second compartment he had taken?" Lucien asked.

"I did," Francine said in a frank tone. "Had I known you were tailing me, I would have been more secretive about my endeavors."

"Now, now, cherie, we both know I could find you anywhere." Lucien breathed out a sardonic laugh, one side of his mouth hitched with a degree of admiration. "So that outburst earlier, that was a charade?"

She pursed her lips and tilted her chin up, as though she was done explaining herself. So, they hadn't been working together. However, there *was* a history between them, a rather complicated one. That was probably why he'd been in her compartment earlier.

"Did you poison Lucien?" Penelope asked, not bothering to put it gently.

Both Francine and Lucien snapped their attention to her. Francine just glowered. Lucien laughed, which meant he didn't think she had.

"Oh, Mademoiselle Banks, I have given her plenty of reason to want me dead before now. This? This is what you Americans call a spat. If anything, I am happy to help her in her endeavors, now that I know she is not after the Golden Monkey. I am quite good at making friends and accomplices...at least temporarily." His eyes sparkled with mischief.

"I am afraid none of this eliminates you as a suspect Mademoiselle, ah, Deschamps. In fact, it only makes you a more likely suspect," Simon said, frowning at Francine, then giving Lucien an equally harsh look. "For now, I will be searching the compartments in the third carriage, Monsieur Barbier's, Monsieur Vollant's, and yours, Mademoiselle."

"I'll go with you," Richard reminded him.

"Of course." Simon pursed his lips as though offended Richard might have been accusing him of something.

When they were gone, Margaret stood from her chair.

"Where are you going?" André stated, suddenly on alert.

"Not that it is any of your business, but I would like to... freshen myself. If that is alright with you?"

André calmed down, but still followed her with wary eyes as she walked to the lavatory. Margaret, already highly agitated, nearly threw a fit when she found the door locked.

"Really, this is all too much! We are down to one for the entirety of the First Class." When Adrien opened the door and exited, making his apologies, she was even more vexed. "Including the staff? At the very least, we should be allowed entry to our compartments for this sort of thing."

Poor Adrien looked mortified, bowing his head apologetically as he scurried over to stand with the other concierges. Both Jules and Quentin gave him sympathetic looks. Penelope also sympathized. The lounge restroom was probably the only one available to the concierges. Now they would have to share it with all the First Class passengers, and of course the two officers pulled from Second Class. She was glad she hadn't needed to use the facilities yet; that was another benefit of not drinking.

"I dare say, now that the subject has been brought up, I feel the need myself."

"Benny really, that's hardly an appropriate topic." Cousin Cordelia wrinkled her nose.

"There are still a few hours to go before we reach

Lyon," Lulu said. "Things are going to get even messier than they already are if we all have to remain here."

"Think of it this way, we are in France. Even the ever elegant Marie Antoinette had to use a pot. I'm sure we can suffice with an ice bucket should it come to that," Benny said.

"Or simply open a window," Honorine said with a laugh. "I remember when things were like that in certain parts of Paris."

"Oh really, now. This is all too much." Cousin Cordelia looked as though she would faint from revulsion.

Penelope bit back a smile, then attempted to reassure her cousin. "Once they search the compartments, perhaps they will let people back into them. At the very least, our car isn't a crime scene."

"I certainly hope you will be requesting a full refund, Penelope dear. This is unacceptable. A murder? An attempted murder? Blackmarket dealings? A flimflam artist? This isn't the sort of thing that should happen in First Class. It's enough to have my nerves unraveling as we speak," Cousin Cordelia fanned herself.

"I'd say First Class is the perfect setting for a grift," Lulu said. "At least folks here have money."

That only had Cousin Cordelia frowning further.

"Speaking of the grift, do we believe anything said thus far?" Benny asked. "What say you, Pen? Honorine, dove?"

"I've had a few suspicions satisfied," Honorine said in a pensive tone. "Though, I don't think we have the full truth yet."

"Oh?" Benny leaned forward, a greedy look in his eyes. "Who remains the liar?"

"I think it awfully interesting that Monsieur Vollant did not succumb to his bit of poisoning."

Penelope turned to view Lucien, who now sat alone, facing the window with a thoughtful frown on his face. Was he worried about what Simon and Richard might find in his compartment, despite his seeming lack of concern about a search? Perhaps all the secrets uncovered had interfered with his plans somehow.

She slid her eyes to Pierre Padou. His gaze remained on his book that had been placed on the bar where André had left it after taking it. If he was thinking of somehow swiping it without anyone noticing it, he was mad. Where would he even hide something that size?

That sparked a sudden thought. "How big is the Golden Monkey of Kashmir?"

Penelope hadn't asked the question to anyone in particular, but there were at least a few people who could answer. One in particular had actually handled it. She settled her gaze on Pierre, who finally answered.

"Not very big at all. Only about fifteen centimeters tall, perhaps eight wide; about the size of a Swiss note."

"So small?" Penelope had expected something larger considering the trouble it had caused.

"Much ado over nothing," Benny hummed.

"That *nothing* may very well be worth more than this train," Lucien retorted, giving the room a look of disdain.

"And as far as we know, it is still here," Honorine said, deliberately making her tone ominous.

"So where is it?" Edward asked, casting a suspicious eye at everyone, certain passengers in particular.

At that moment, Simon and Richard returned, the expressions on their faces were quite telling. Richard looked resigned. Simon looked particularly irate.

"I see the Golden Monkey remains elusive," Lucien said, his sardonic amusement returning.

"Indeed," Simon gritted. "As such, we will be searching the entire First Class train. Anyone who refuses to have their belongings checked will remain in this lounge until we reach Lyon, and formal procedures can commence." The look on his face silenced any protest. "We *will* find the Golden Monkey."

CHAPTER THIRTY

Surprisingly there were few protests at Simon's insistence that everyone's belongings and compartments should be searched for the elusive Golden Monkey of Kashmir. In fact, the only one offered came from Penelope.

"Don't you suppose the murder of Monsieur Barbier should be made a priority?"

At first, a look of incredulity came to Simon's face. It was quickly erased when he realized her statement made perfect sense. "Of course, Mademoiselle. I am simply working under the assumption that whoever has the Golden Monkey is likely to be the murderer."

It was in fact a plausible assumption, but not a comprehensive one. There was still motive to consider. Aristide was like a sheep in a den of wolves while on board. Perhaps not the most apt description, considering he had behaved more like a wolf than anyone, preying on the vulnerable. Still, one couldn't dismiss a motive that was strictly greed.

"However, you do make a good point, now that I think about it, mademoiselle. I believe perhaps another round of questioning." Simon turned to his partner. "We should each take a suspect for brief questioning, determining where they were and when."

André seemed uncertain, or perhaps just impatient to get on with finding the Golden Monkey, but he nodded. "Oui."

Simon turned back to the passengers, narrowing his gaze on one in particular. "I will start with Monsieur Vollant."

"Surely we aren't meant to wait here while you do another round of questioning?" Margaret protested. "Perhaps you have not noticed there is only one freely available..."

She couldn't bring herself to say it, so Edward helpfully finished for her. "Lavatory. And yes, it may become an inconvenience again."

Adrien shifted uncomfortably, his head bowed with embarrassment at having been the cause of such a predicament.

"Is there not another public one in First Class?"

"There are facilities in each compartment."

"No," Simon said quickly. "Not until every floorboard and wall has been ripped out if necessary to find the Golden Monkey."

"Now, see here—" Edward argued, but he was interrupted.

"The interviews will be quick," Simon said, then added with more sympathy, " Perhaps in between interviews, we can do a search. But first, we will talk with Monsieur Vollant and..." he deferred to his partner to pick a suspect.

"Monsieur Padou," André decided, making sure to take hold of the large book with the bonds inside as he did.

Lucien and Pierre, neither having anything to hide it seemed, rose and followed the two officers into the dining room. Through the French doors, which were closed to them, Penelope saw Simon and Lucien take the furthest table for two while André and Pierre took the closest table for four.

Richard took his seat next to Penelope where she still sat with their friends and Honorine.

"Now, now, detective, you didn't abscond with the Golden Monkey while you were searching, did you?" Benny asked with a devilish grin. "I promise not to tell."

Richard gave him an irritated twist of the lips, and didn't bother answering.

"Leave him be, Benny," Cousin Cordelia said. "He is quite possibly the only trustworthy person on this train." She quickly added, "I, of course, am not including all of you." She flashed an apologetic smile, though Pen didn't miss the way her eyes very briefly darted with speculation to Honorine.

"So, it wasn't in any of the compartments?" Pen asked.

"We searched every one of them. I, myself, searched Lucien's while he took Mademoiselle Cochet's, I mean Mademoiselle Deschamps, I suppose. It's getting difficult to keep up with everyone's name change."

"Of course it is, dear," Cousin Cordelia said. "None of us have had a decent night's sleep at all. It's appalling! Whatever are we to do when we reach Paris?"

"We'll be there for at least a month, Cousin. I'm sure one day of rest to recover won't ruin it." Pen said, then turned back to Richard. He looked as exhausted as she felt. It had been a long night, and most people had only gotten a wink of sleep, if that. The excitement of the murder, theft, and then attempted murder was beginning to wear off.

She looked into the dining room again. Simon leaned in, his face practically red with anger as he interrogated

Lucien, who also leaned in, probably defending himself. Whatever screws Simon was attaching to his thumbs had succeeded in snuffing out that insouciant attitude of his. Perhaps he was just frustrated at having the finger pointed his way. If Richard had searched his room, then the Golden Monkey most certainly wasn't there. Her cousin was correct in her assessment that he was the most trustworthy, at least when it came to the police on board. André was easily hot-tempered, but young, so perhaps that would eventually cool. Simon seemed level-headed enough, though not at the moment. Penelope sympathized. It must have been frustrating to not only lose the target you were after to murder (which was as yet unsolved) but also the very artifact you were hoping to reclaim. Unless the thief was reckless or desperate enough to throw it off the train, the Golden Monkey of Kashmir had to be on board somewhere.

So where was it?

Penelope glanced at Lucien and Simon, who no longer seemed to be in a heated exchange. Simon still looked angry, or rather frustrated. Lucien's back was to her, so she couldn't see his expression.

Penelope considered something for a moment before coming to a decision. She didn't want to discuss what was on her mind in front of the others, at least not until she had talked to Richard who could offer the most expert opinion.

"Can I talk to you in private?" He looked alarmed and she quickly added, "About a theory I have." That only had him sporting a wry expression, but he nodded and followed her into a private corner. Pen ignored all the suspicious eyes that followed them.

"What is it you wanted to ask?"

"How did the two of you decide who searched which room?"

Richard caught on to what she was saying instantly. "He suggested I search Lucien's room. It seemed appropriate at the time. Why?"

"Nothing," Pen said, not wanting to make an accusation when all she had was a theory.

Richard was not to be deterred. "No, you're thinking of something. What is it? Do you suppose sending me to Lucien's compartment was a ruse?"

"I'm not sure," Pen said, feeling her frustration set in. What was she missing? "I just...it seems odd that André would storm away somehow not realizing Lucien wasn't in fact dead."

"Simon did seem fairly upset about that, rightfully so."

"Unless it was an act. It was rather interesting that he would have you search Lucien's room the one and only time it's been searched. Perhaps he knew the Golden Monkey wasn't there?"

Richard arched a brow. "Or, perhaps he trusts me."

"And who wouldn't, darling?" Pen said with a reassuring smile. "It's just that, it isn't even your case."

"Perhaps he wanted an air of legitimacy. Accusations had been tossed around about corrupt officers. Could it be that he just wanted to make sure it was all above suspicion?"

"Or, again, he knew there was nothing to be found in there? After all Lucien had said as much. Perhaps that was a signal."

Richard turned to glance at Simon and Lucien, then back to Penelope. "Do you think they are all conspiring to steal the Golden Monkey?"

"I think everything has been awfully convenient. At the very least, Lucien's *supposed* poisoning was a surprising little intermission to this murder-cum-theft."

"And also very convenient. Alright, let's suppose you

are onto something. It would beg the question, was it planned or a spontaneous bit of deception?"

"It could still be a legitimate case of attempted murder?" Pen offered, just to see if he would take the bait.

He smiled. "I do love how we always play devil's advocate with one another."

She smiled back. "It does help solve cases faster."

He became serious again. "Alright, if we're going to do this, let's think of means and opportunity. Heaven knows we already have motive. Where would he have gotten the poison?"

"If there even was poison. Many things could mimic foaming at the mouth. I've blown a bubble or two from having my mouth washed out with soap."

"I'm sure you did, my dear." Richard chuckled softly, then became thoughtful again. "As always, it's a matter of what can be proven."

"Let's look at each scenario in turn. If Lucien was working on his own, it *would* have to be quite fortuitous that he was left alone. Perhaps the self-poisoning was simply an attempt to remove the suspicion of murder from himself. Then, when he discovered he had the car to himself he simply took advantage. He's certainly shown himself to be the opportunistic sort."

"True. He's also the smart sort. He would have known everyone's belongings would be searched. Besides, he was supposedly after the Golden Monkey to earn the finder's fee, not to steal it. What would be the point of going to this much trouble, knowing the police would search him and his belongings before he even stepped off the train? They'd confiscate it and he'd not only have no finder's fee, he'd be arrested for theft, possibly murder."

"He *claims* earning the finder's fee was his intention. Do you trust him at his word?"

Richard's skeptical expression said everything.

"There then. However, there is one person we can probe to learn more. Someone who may still be after the Golden Monkey herself."

They both turned to where Francine sat. She was already boring a hole into them with her gaze as though she knew exactly what they wanted to ask her.

CHAPTER THIRTY-ONE

Richard and Penelope took Francine's stare directed their way as an invitation to walk over and question her. Again, curious eyes followed them.

"Go on then, I assume you want to interrogate me further. I have nothing more to reveal, I'm afraid," Francine said.

"Actually, Mademoiselle....Deschamps? Or should I continue to call you Cosette Cochet?"

She gave him a cool look. "As I said, I have nothing more to reveal. You know everything, including my real name. I am Francine Deschamps and I would prefer to go by that name."

"Of course," Richard said, clearing his throat. He and Penelope pulled chairs closer to her and sat down.

"It isn't you we wanted to discuss. It's your friend, Lucien."

"Lucien does not have friends. Nor do I. He is—*was* a mentor of sorts. I knew better than to get too close to him. You can see how avaricious he is, and the means to which he is willing to go. As I stated, a scorpion does not change."

"Which is why we wanted to ask you, do you believe he was really here to find the Golden Monkey of Kashmir to return to the rightful owner for a reward or finder's fee? It could be sold for much more on the blackmarket."

Francine laughed lightly and shook her head. "There is one thing Lucien loves more than money, more than winning. That is his own neck. He would never risk it by dipping his toe too far into the criminal world." An enigmatic yet cynical smile came to her lips. "After all, it's far more lucrative to make friends in the criminal *pursuit* world."

Penelope and Richard glanced at one another, then back to Francine.

"So he has friends in the police?"

"Of course. It can be quite helpful." A sour twist came to her lips. "And they never require more of him than a game of cards or round of drinks. Though, more often, it's a portion of the reward. The police are not allowed to collect, you see."

Of course they weren't. That made Lucien's arrangement a mutually beneficial relationship. One he may have contrived prior to boarding. Or, as he was wont to do, he simply took advantage of an opportunity while on board. Penelope wasn't the only one who suddenly came to that conclusion. Richard frowned, his opinion of André and Simon suddenly tainted.

"Could he be working with one of the international policemen, perhaps both?" It wasn't a question and Francine didn't need to answer. They were all thinking the same thing.

Instead, Pen turned to Richard. "Did anything strike you as odd, or perhaps even a little too accommodating while you were searching? Other than Simon allowing you to search Lucien's room?"

Francine snorted with derision upon hearing that, and shot him a patronizing smile, as though that should have been a clue that something was amiss.

Richard's jaw hardened and his gaze cooled toward her before he continued. "It doesn't matter, as nothing was found."

"But—"

"I performed my own search of every cabin after him, just to be sure. He was rightfully offended, but I don't compromise when it comes to murder."

Penelope couldn't help but beam with admiration. She noted Francine do the same, to a lesser, more cynical degree.

"Could either of them have hidden it on themselves, perhaps in a pocket or underneath his jacket? It's quite small, it seems, so that could be a possibility." Pen was beginning to think perhaps the Golden Monkey had come to life and wandered off the train on its own at that point.

Richard shook his head. "The anger and frustration on Simon's face was genuine."

"Perhaps that response was that of someone who didn't find the missing Monkey...when they fully expected they would?" Penelope was still leaving open the option that Lucien had been communicating in code when he told Simon the Golden Monkey wasn't in his compartment.

Richard considered Penelope's suggestion. "Perhaps."

"Oh for heaven's sake, I want a drink!" Margaret suddenly erupted, drawing everyone's attention.

Penelope turned to find her shaking off Edward's restraining hand and storming to the bar. "In fact, I think I might finally take advantage of the free champagne while I'm imprisoned on this train. I know you have at least one open bottle back there." She flung her hand in Honorine's direction. *"That one* has been drinking it like water all evening." She then flung her hand Quentin's way. "He knows that better than anyone."

Quentin balked at being included in her little tirade. He certainly didn't confirm Honorine's champagne habit one way or another, standing more erect to present a solid front. Jules, standing next to him, did the same in solidarity. Adrien was missing, presumably using the lavatory yet again. Penelope could only wonder why a woman who had been so vociferous about limited facilities for so many passengers would want to drink any more than necessary. It seemed all the more insensible as both interviews in the dining room seemed to be going much longer than Simon claimed they would.

Just as she turned her head to see if there was any indication the interviews might be coming to a conclusion, she saw Lucien shoot up from his seat. He stood there, straightening his jacket as he gave some parting words to Simon before turning on his heels and stalking out of the dining car. His face was pure granite, but there was worry and frustration coloring his eyes. Penelope could see Simon looking perfectly surprised, then perfectly irate in his wake. André snatched his eyes away from Pierre and followed, his expression remaining bewildered.

"How do you plan on learning the truth of it?" Penelope snapped her eyes back to Francine, who was leaning in, her arms draped over her crossed leg as she addressed Pen, staring with cat-like eyes. "Lucien is an expert in the art of deception. He will not be so easily—"

"Oh, *applesauce!*" Pen interrupted. She shot up from

her chair and strode over. Lucien was caught by surprise by the sudden act, and it remained the only expression on his face by the time she reached him. Which was perfect for her purposes. "Are you, Simon, and André working together to steal the Golden Monkey?"

CHAPTER THIRTY-TWO

P enelope had learned a lot early on during her years of playing poker to make money. Anyone who even dared start a game knew it was not a game of chance but a game of deceit, risk, and, yes, doing the unexpected. Catching your opponent by surprise allowed a brief window of opportunity where you could see their honest emotions.

Lucien wasn't the only one who was a master of deceit.

He was also a flawed poker player.

"What?" Like a cat startled by a sudden noise, he flinched. Down went his mask, and wide with alarm went his eyes.

"You *are*?" Pen was almost as surprised that she had been right.

Like a spring trap, his mask of sly indifference came back. Rather than answer, he simply pulled out his cigarette case and plucked one out to slip into his mouth. He leaned ever so slightly toward her, a subtle smile curling the lips that held the cigarette. Lucien knew she didn't like the smell of it and was hoping to taunt her to go away—and leave the question alone while she was at it.

"What is happening?" André was the first to storm out, having heard Pen's frank question to Lucien. Pierre was all but forgotten, along with his book, which still sat on the table in front of him. "What did you just ask him?"

"A question which Monsieur Vollant was foolish enough to answer," Honorine answered for Pen.

Lucien sighed, then lazily removed his cigarette. "I did no such thing."

"What did you tell her?" André spat, certainly not taking him at his word.

Pen found the choice of question interesting. It wasn't "What did you say?" but "What did you tell her?"

"Nothing," Lucine insisted, becoming exasperated. Even he knew André had erred with that phrasing.

"She is just trying to create a distraction," Simon said, strolling out into the lounge area looking perfectly unconcerned. "Mademoiselle Banks, your accusations have been made without proof or a confession." He turned to arch a questioning brow at Lucien.

"Précisément," Lucien said, though Pen detected a hint of wariness to it. He put his cigarette back into his mouth and pulled out his lighter. At first, she thought his failure to get it to spark was his nervousness kicking in, all but confirming he was shaken by her accusation—perhaps from guilt? However, he cursed and snatched the cigarette away, then glared at Honorine. "How often did you use my lighter? It's nearly out of fluid!"

"*Moi*? Why must I be guilty of everything tonight?" Honorine asked. Her tone was light, but Penelope sensed a hint of irritation in her voice.

"Allow me, Monsieur." Jules, who was the closest

concierge, rushed to assist him. He pulled out a blue box of matches similar to that Mica had earlier given to Lucien.

Lucien must have forgotten he had his own box of matches. He was still either rattled or frustrated by Penelope's accusation, which was evidenced by how long it took for him to steady his cigarette. The match was burned nearly to Jules's fingers by the time it was lit, but he hid the pain of the heat well. Still, his jaw was quite taut when he shook the match—perhaps a little too hurriedly—to extinguish the flame.

It wasn't lost on Lucien who arched a brow of apology. "Now, you know why I prefer my lighter."

"Enough with your lighter and cigarette," André snapped. "An accusation has been made, and it must be addressed."

"We have our priorities, André," Simon said in a pointed tone. He turned to give Penelope a piercing look. "The Golden Monkey is still missing."

"Is it?" Honorine was daring enough to ask. "Of course you would say that if you had been the one to steal it." She cast a twinkling eye toward Lucien. "With help perhaps?"

"Another false accusation. Perhaps André and I will have to file a civil charge for sullying our reputation?"

"A simple search of your belongings when we arrive to Lyon should quell the rumor. Or perhaps Paris? As you stated, I'm very well known among the police there. They wouldn't dismiss such a suggestion so lightly if it came from *moi*."

Simon stared at her for a long time, as though he could erode her insolence simply with a harsh gaze. A humorless smile appeared on his face. "That would not matter, of course. As I stated, the Golden Monkey is still missing."

Simon was acting far too unconcerned about a possible

search of his things. Either he, in conspiracy with Lucien, had hidden the Golden Monkey too well, or they really didn't have it. Lucien looked put out, as though disappointed he hadn't found it. André still scowled with anger at the accusation, but Pen could see the concern coloring his eyes. Was he the one with whom Lucien had been conspiring? It made sense, as he'd been the one in the same carriage when Lucien had supposedly succumbed to poisoning. Still, there was one tiny problem that had been bothering Penelope, and now seemed far more pressing. Perhaps even the very thing that might provide proof.

"Adrien." Penelope had announced his name so abruptly that the poor concierge, now out of the lavatory, started in surprise. He stared at her with wary eyes and Pen felt bad, remembering how besieged he'd been all night. "You have a master key to all the compartments, no?"

"I do," he said cautiously.

"Is it on you now?"

His brow wrinkled in confusion, but his hand instantly went up to the inside of his jacket to retrieve it from the same little chain she'd seen Quentin have on his person when he opened Monsieur Barbier's compartment. Adrien's eyes went suddenly wide as though shocked to realize his wasn't there.

"I...I don't know where—"

"*Adrien, have you lost it?*" Quentin hissed, sotto voce in French, though most in the lounge could still hear it.

"No, he didn't," Penelope confirmed, then for his benefit, quickly continued, "Lucien has it."

Lucien's expression of surprised indignation was almost laughable. As it was, a few people did cough out a laugh. That dissolved his pretense and a subtle smile came to his face.

Penelope explained. "One thing that bothered me about my accusation was how quickly you could have searched so many of the rooms before your reappearance. Having dabbled in picking locks, I can attest to how time-consuming it can be. However, one with a master key could avoid such delays. You had plenty of time to yourself, conveniently enough," she cast a quick glance to Simon and André, before addressing Lucien again. "However, your fellow passengers were bound to get impatient to return to their compartments. Some might flagrantly ignore any instructions to remain here, which wouldn't work well for you if you were caught in the act."

Penelope stopped, waiting for a response from any of them. Lucien simply stared at her for a few seconds, then idly slid his eyes to Simon and André. They both remained staunchly quiet.

"Monsieur Vollant, if you have the master key, I must insist that you return it. Otherwise, I will have to get the conductor, who will demand that—"

"*Sacre bleu*," Lucien said with sardonic exaggeration. He pulled out the key from his pocket. "Here is your key." He gave Honorine a devilish smile before adding, "I *found* it."

Several impassioned people spoke at once.

"What are you doing?" André hissed in anger.

"Just how many compartments did you search, and whose?" Francine asked.

"Unacceptable," Jules said.

"Yes, it is," Quentin agreed, encouraging Adrien to retrieve his key.

"It seems we have another thief to burn at the stake, *non*?" Honorine mused.

Adrien, looking abashed once again scurried over to

retrieve his key. Penelope felt even worse for him. His only sin was to have been delegated to the third First Class car. He probably thought his duties would be lighter, catering to only two people. Now, he was guaranteed a reprimand for having allowed this to happen.

"Yes, we do have a thief," Richard said, his tone indicating he also felt bad for Adrien. "You do realize this at least warrants an arrest once we reach Lyon, Monsieur Vollant?"

"*Au contraire*," Lucien replied with a rather smug smile. "I do not think I will be arrested for anything."

There was silence on the heels of that, everyone wondering what he meant, and more importantly, why he seemed so certain.

"Because you have been working with at least one of the two men from the International Criminal Police Commission," Penelope said. She turned to Simon and André, who did their best to remain impassive, but she could sense the caution in their eyes as she continued. "You wanted an easy way to steal the Golden Monkey for yourself. So you used the services of an expert. In fact, I'd be willing to bet it was one of you who stole the key."

"That is an outrageous lie! You have no—"

"Calm down," Simon said, patiently but sternly. He narrowed his eyes at Penelope. "She is baiting you, you fool."

André didn't appreciate the insult.

"Yes, I am sorry, but your partner is right, I was baiting you. Unnecessarily, I should add. Lucien seems certain that he will not end up in prison, or even arrested. Which means he was working with you." She could see André going tense again. "I think you availed yourself of his expertise to avoid any irritating legal obstacles like warrants and probable cause. You've been rather careless with your searches thus far. To make a proper, and more importantly, successful arrest, you'd need to play by the rules. However, a citizen, especially one with few scruples, left alone to his own devices, wouldn't be bound by any such rules. He could get the finder's reward and you would get a feather in your cap for having solved such an important case."

"Précisément," Honorine said, mimicking Lucien.

The low laugh that escaped his lips confirmed Penelope's theory was correct.

"I do not know why you are laughing," André spat. "The artifact is still missing."

"Indeed it is," Simon announced. He gave Penelope one lingering, harsh look before he exhaled and spun to face everyone else in the room. "Which returns us to the most important question of this tragic voyage, who killed Aristide Barbier?" He turned to Penelope and then Honorine. "No more of your amateur detecting. André and I will handle this until we reach Lyon and it can be turned over to the proper authorities. We have only a few hours until we reach that stop. Until then, we will all remain here in the lounge. If you feel tired, then sleep where you sit. Take your objections up with the company. A murderer is still among us and a priceless artifact is still on board the train. I intend to uncover both before the night is over."

CHAPTER THIRTY-THREE

On the heels of Simon's instruction that everyone was to remain in the lounge, there seemed to be a collective cloud of exhaustion that claimed the passengers. Even the poor concierges looked weary, as though they wanted nothing more than to return to the normal routine of serving demanding passengers. No one offered any protest, even Margaret, who sipped her champagne—there had, in fact, been an open bottle—in sullen silence.

Penelope and Richard had returned to their seats with the others. The lack of sleep was beginning to show, but the excitement of a murder case still gleamed in their eyes.

"Surely you are not going to be so obedient," Honorine goaded. "Who are they to keep us from investigating?"

"Well...I certainly can't help what happens in my head," Penelope hedged, shrugging as though her inquisitive nature was a faucet she had no power to turn off.

"Need I remind you both that there is a murderer among us?"

"My dear Richard, surely you know the woman you are going to marry by now," Benny crooned.

"I do, which is why I know it will be pointless to tell her what to do when it comes to anything." Richard at least managed a smile. "In fact, I'm interested to know exactly what *is* happening in her head."

Penelope wriggled with satisfaction in her seat and sat up straighter as she considered her thoughts. "Again, it really comes down to the timeline, specifically any windows of opportunity someone may have had to steal the Golden Monkey, and presumably kill Aristide at the same time."

"But which Golden Monkey?" Lulu pointed out.

"*Exactement*," Honorine said with a grin. "If we are to believe Monsieur Padou, there was a fake Golden Monkey left in his room after he returned from dinner."

"Which means the real one was stashed away somewhere before then."

"But only after Pierre returned to the dining room," Richard said. "He was originally given the real one."

"Yes," Penelope said, briefly nibbling her thumb in thought. "So, did Aristide move the real one or did someone else?"

"Either is a possibility," Lulu said. "But only if you believe him when he says that man was dead when he placed the fake Golden Monkey in his compartment. Aristide could have moved the real one, then someone later came by to murder him. Or someone stole it and killed him in the act of stealing it."

Penelope sighed. "That does nothing to narrow down the list of suspects. We know that the window of opportunity extends to after the dinner service, as Quentin was not at his station then." She turned to give Honorine an apologetic look. "That still includes you as a suspect, I'm afraid."

"*Naturellement*," Honorine said, as though that was to

be expected. Her mouth twisted as she eyed everyone, reminding them that they too were suspects, in that case.

"Let's take each scenario in turn," Richard suggested. "We'll start with the assumption that Monsieur Barbier moved the real Golden Monkey himself. Where would he have moved it?"

"More importantly, why has no one found it yet?" Benny said, sounding almost as exasperated as Simon had been.

"Because he hid it well?" Even Penelope could hear the doubt in her own voice.

Honorine sensed it and met her with a keen look. "And he knows the train so well? All the hiding places, such that even an experienced thief and the police cannot find it?" She clucked her tongue, dismissing the idea.

"It does make sense that he simply moved it to his second compartment. Perhaps that's the reason he had the second compartment. He knew he would be switching out the Golden Monkeys. In fact, he would not have even needed to hide it, as he would have been under the assumption that no one would have even discovered a second one."

"Except *Monsieur Padou* certainly did," Lulu said, one eyebrow arched.

"But when would he have moved it?" Benny asked. "Quentin and the questionably close siblings," he took a moment to smirk at his own little jab, "all claim they either saw or heard him in his compartment."

"There was a brief window when Quentin was gone to retrieve his dinner tray. In fact, he may have sent him for that very reason," Richard said.

"But then surely Adrien would have seen him entering the third car." Penelope turned to see if she could get

Adrien's attention, but it seemed the concierge had once again dismissed himself to use the lavatory.

"My goodness, the man is practically a sieve," Benny hummed.

"And when have you ever been close enough to a kitchen to have seen a sieve?" Lulu teased.

"I'll have you know, I have actually been below stairs, dove."

"Is that so?"

Benny glared. "That wasn't a euphemism for slumming."

"Do you two mind if we focus on the murder case?" Pen asked.

"Benjamin does make a good point," Honorine said. "It is very likely that Adrien was away from his post at the time Aristide placed the real Golden Monkey in his compartment."

At that moment, the door opened and Adrien stepped out to rejoin the other concierges. Penelope rethought her original idea of calling him over. She briefly turned to see Simon and André were preoccupied with giving a perfectly unconcerned Lucien an earful. Loudly asking Adrien to join them would only rouse their suspicion.

"I'm going to go and talk to him by myself," Pen said, standing up before any of them could protest. She kept watch over Simon, André, and Lucien, if only to make sure they were preoccupied. Fortunately, they were still talking when she caught up to Adrien. He saw her approach and his eyes widened slightly with panic before he collected himself.

"I wondered if I might ask you a question."

Quentin and Jules both creased their brows with concern for their fellow concierge, as though they knew

Penelope was about to make trouble. Pen ignored them and focused on Adrien.

"Of course, how can I be of service Mademoiselle Banks?" Adrien asked.

"I..." Penelope considered how she could pose her question in a delicate way. "I was just wondering, if you saw Monsieur Barbier leave his compartment in the second carriage to visit his compartment in the third carriage at any point during the dinner service, or really at any point after dinner began?"

His eyelids flickered, then he forced a professional smile on his face. "No, mademoiselle, I did not."

"I see." Penelope paused just to make it seem like she was satisfied with that answer, then pretended to suddenly think of a subsequent question. "Perhaps you were away from your station in the third car, even if only briefly?"

He hesitated, and Penelope was about to take back the question. She certainly had no desire to embarrass him, even if it meant solving a murder case or finding the Golden Monkey. The authorities would be asking the same questions soon enough. However, Jules stepped in to offer an adequate explanation.

"Dinner service is when we often handle housekeeping or administrative duties, such as turning down the beds in the compartments. There are usually no passengers that need seeing to, so it is a convenient time to take care of such things. Of course, there is always at least one concierge on duty, no matter what. That is what the call system is for. It reaches all of us, and of course, we are all alerted when any of us leaves our station, even momentarily."

"Of course," Penelope said, matching his smile. "That is certainly reassuring. Thank you."

"What are you discussing?" Simon had finally taken

note of Penelope conversing with the concierges. His eyes were narrowed with suspicion. Lucien had left and was sitting with Francine once again. "Are you interfering with this case, Mademoiselle Banks?"

"No, I..." Penelope thought quickly. "I was simply inquiring about something to eat. If you insist that we remain in the lounge without sleep, we should at least be afforded a bit of refreshment. Particularly since you are limiting our alcohol intake."

Simon scrutinized her, unsure whether to believe her or not.

"We can, of course," Adrien quickly said, playing along. "It would not be a problem. We are quite used to procuring after-dinner requests, and the kitchen is always staffed and well-stocked."

"I suppose there is no harm in that. From now on, all requests must be approved by either my partner or myself." He nodded at Adrien. "You and....Jules may procure something from the kitchen for all of us. Be quick about it."

Jules and Adrien left. Quentin offered her an appreciative smile at not revealing his fellow concierge's secret. "That was gracious of you, Mademoiselle Banks," he whispered. "We are both rather protective of Adrien. He has taught Jules and I so much, so we are quite grateful to him. He worked on the Orient Express, you know."

"Did he?" Penelope was impressed.

"Oui." Quentin seemed to realize that fact invited the most obvious questions, namely, why he had switched to the present line, not that it was anything to turn one's nose up to. "We are all fortunate to have these positions, of course. Jules is saving money to get married soon, and I..." His smile faltered and his gaze flickered with concern. "I am taking care of my father."

"Is he ill?"

"He..." His eyes went wide with alarm, realizing he was breaking some cardinal rule for concierges. "I apologize, Mademoiselle Banks, that was....he is fine."

Penelope could tell from the troubled look in his eyes that his father was not fine, but she wasn't about to put another concierge in an uncomfortable position by insisting on details.

"Of course, and thank you, Quentin."

"Oui, Mademoiselle Banks," He said with a note of relief in his voice.

Penelope walked back to sit with her friends, thinking over what little she had learned. She suspected Adrien had been dismissed from the Orient Express for his habitual use of the facilities. What good was a concierge if he was often away from his station? She thought it kind that Quentin and Jules were so quick to protect him. However, that may have very well given the murderer or thief, perhaps one and the same, their window of opportunity. Though none of the concierges had actually stated it, it was heavily implied that Adrien hadn't been at his station during the entire period of dinner service. With him gone, Quentin attending to Aristide's dinner, and Jules in the first car, where he wouldn't have seen Aristide pass, it was entirely possible that he could have taken the real Golden Monkey to his compartment unnoticed.

"We have a window of opportunity," Pen announced when she sat back down. "There was very likely a period during dinner when Aristide could have taken the real Golden Monkey to his compartment in the third carriage."

"I'm afraid that only creates another mystery," Richard said. "There are a few likely suspects in the theft of that particular Golden Monkey, most likely Lucien and

Francine who were in that same third carriage. Monsieur Padou is an even more likely suspect." Richard turned to view him, still sitting at a table in the dining room with his precious book still on the table before him. "However, that doesn't necessarily mean any of them killed Monsieur Barbier or took the second Golden Monkey."

"I suppose I should defend myself and state once again that it was not I who took either the fake Golden Monkey, the real one, or who killed Monsieur Barbier," Honorine said with a heavy sigh, as though prepared for the protests.

"I suppose, though...I do have one question," Penelope said, now that the opportunity had presented itself. "Why steal Lucien's lighter rather than simply get a match from one of the concierges?"

The smile on Honorine's face was almost patronizing. "It is fair to think that I am an insatiable thief. Yes, I stole Aristide's wallet but then returned it to him, if you recall. Contrary to Lucien's claims, I did not steal his lighter. I found it, which was rather convenient for my purposes. Asking Quentin or another concierge for a match might have incurred...*unwanted* curiosity. After all, I am not a smoker. Finding Lucien's lighter, I had no need to arouse any curiosity about my intended purpose."

Penelope frowned. At that point, Honorine had little reason to lie about such a trifle. There was still one question, though. "Where did you find it?"

"It was in the passageway between carriages."

"Which carriages?"

"The third and second. *Pourquoi?*"

Penelope didn't have an immediate answer, but instead pondered that information and how it fit with everything else. After a moment, she realized there was one individual that tied everything up rather neatly.

CHAPTER THIRTY-FOUR

"The lighter, does it mean anything?" Honorine pressed. She stared at Penelope intently, as though she could fathom an answer if she pierced her with her gaze hard enough.

"I think...it might mean everything. Of course, that really depends."

"Oh, enough with the mystery, dove," Benny said with impatience. He shot a daring grin Pen's way. "You have a suspect, don't you?"

"I may," she cast a look toward the individual she had in mind. All eyes followed her gaze. "The only problem is, it will be difficult to get him to talk."

"Lucien?" Honorine said, twisting around to get a better look.

Lucien's back was to them where he sat with Francine. She was the first to notice Penelope and her friends staring their way. She said something to him and he turned his head to view them. Lucien's brow lowered with confusion and dismay, then smoothed out as his sly smile came back. He arched a questioning brow.

Penelope stood up.

"You're going to talk to him?" Richard objected. "If you suspect he's the murderer, I don't think that's a good idea."

"There isn't much he can possibly do here in front of everyone, darling. If I'm right, he'll be in handcuffs when we reach Lyon. And before you suggest coming with me, we both know how that would unfold. Just trust me, Richard."

He relaxed, but his expression indicated he wasn't happy about it. It was very sweet that he worried so about her. However, Penelope wasn't quite at the stage for pointing fingers. She had exactly one question for him that would determine guilt or innocence.

"Where are you going?"

Penelope sighed, irritated by Simon's meddling presence. Yes, she was technically interfering in the investigation, but really, it was all for the greater good. She was far more likely to be of help than a hindrance.

"I'm just going to ask something of Lucien."

Simon's eyes narrowed. "And what is that?"

"His lighter." She arched a brow, daring Simon to find fault with that answer.

His mouth tightened with displeasure, knowing something mischievous was afoot, however he couldn't very well object to such a seemingly innocuous request. He grumbled then jerked his head, giving Penelope permission to proceed. She felt his eyes on her the rest of the way.

"Do not tell me you also have correspondence to burn?" Lucien said, an amused hitch in his mouth. "Perhaps some *lettres d'amour* you do not want your fiancé to find? We both know you do not smoke."

Penelope pursed her lips. "I simply wanted to ask when you last used it and where."

He frowned in confusion, not expecting that question.

His brow furrowed even more as he thought about it, then deepened as he wondered why Penelope wanted to know.

Pen realized a bit of deception on her part was necessary. Frankly, it was only fair considering her target. She leaned in with a conspiratorial smile. "I have a theory about Honorine. I suspect she may have stolen it, contrary to what she claims. I know you had a cigarette during dinner. Is that when you last used your lighter and subsequently lost it?"

"*Non*," he shook his head. "I meant to use it then, but that's when I discovered it was missing."

"Did you search for it?"

"*Bien sûr*," he shrugged.

"Where?"

Penelope could see his growing impatience as he answered. "My compartment, *naturellement*, the corridor, Adrien's station—I thought perhaps he had found it and put it there for safekeeping—and the lounge."

"Not the passageways? The one between the first and second cars is where I first saw you smoking a cigarette."

A devilish smile lifted one side of his mouth. "I was... curious about my fellow travelers."

"Don't lie," Francine said. "He saw Aristide leave the compartment in the third car and followed him into the second."

Lucien laughed softly. "Oui, I followed him, then continued to the passageway between the second and first car to smoke, so as not to arouse suspicion."

"And during dinner?" Penelope continued. "You mentioned you had requested a light from Mica. Why not one of the concierges?"

His face wrinkled with irritation at the barrage of questions, but he answered. "Adrien was not at his station." He arched a brow and his mouth twisted to the side, as though that had been an irritating constant throughout the voyage. "I saw no reason to go all the way to the second car when the bar was right here."

"So the only time you smoked in the passageway between the first and second carriages was when I passed by you just after we left Nice?"

"*Oui.*" He nodded.

Penelope felt her heart quicken. She took a moment to recall her walk from dinner back to her compartment. There had been a lingering scent of cigarette smoke in the corridor of the second carriage. She had assumed that was Aristide, smoking in his compartment. However, the scent had only gotten stronger as she neared the first carriage, further away from his compartment.

"Are you still asking to borrow a lighter, Mademoiselle Banks?"

Penelope jumped at the sound of Simon's voice behind her. She hadn't heard him approach, as she'd been so consumed with getting information. She spun around and plastered a smile on her face.

"No, no, I am done."

At that moment Jules and Adrien returned with trays of food. Plates with an array of cheeses, olives, and tiny finger sandwiches were placed on each. It was an impressive display, considering it had all been made on demand only minutes ago.

Adrien brought a tray to their little grouping, placing a plate on the small table between Lucien and Francine.

"Thank you, Adrien," Penelope said, smiling broadly.

"Of course, mademoiselle," he replied, matching her smile just as broadly. He was probably relieved that she had nothing more to ask of him.

"No more questions," Penelope briskly said, offering a

pert smile to Simon. She quickly returned to her friends. Jules was setting several plates down on the small side tables near them. She offered a dazzling smile to him as well. Just the sight of so much food seemed to make her ravenous again, despite the heavy dinner. She was glad her impromptu request, which had really been nothing more than a ruse for her little interrogation had such a convenient benefit. "Thank you for this, Jules."

"Of course, Mademoiselle Banks." His smile was pleasant and professional.

"I'm surprised the kitchen staff was able to assemble such an array so quickly. Please give them my thanks."

"Of course, Mademoiselle Banks." He offered another quick, close-lipped smile, which was the same one he'd offered during the entire train voyage.

Penelope leaned in, peering closely as though noticing something. Jules's brow wrinkled. "Is there a problem, mademoiselle?"

She urged him closer and he leaned in. "I thought I saw something on your teeth," she whispered.

Jules looked aghast at such an embarrassing faux pas. She watched him discreetly run his tongue over his teeth behind his closed mouth. When he was done she peered in closer.

"Ahh," she hummed, her eyes peering into his mouth. That at last had the intended effect of having him show his teeth as he gave her a questioning look. They were quite stained with a yellowish tinge.

Penelope pulled back and stared at him, realizing she had just potentially solved the case. "You're a smoker."

"I..." Jules blinked in surprise at the statement, then attained a professional demeanor. "We are forbidden from smoking while in service, Mademoiselle Banks."

By then, everyone in their little group had temporarily forgotten about the freshly placed plates of food. They realized Penelope was unraveling an important clue.

"Of course." Penelope gave him a pitying look. "That is perhaps why you took advantage during dinner service. You used the passageway in the hopes that it would avoid placing any suspicion on you via the smell of it."

"And in the corridor of the second car," Richard said, the realization suddenly coloring his expression. "It wasn't Monsieur Barbier smoking in his room that Edward and Margaret smelled, it was you."

"*Mon dieu,*" Honorine whispered. "You are the one who killed Aristide."

Instinctively, the others on the couch, Lulu, Cousin Cordelia, and Benny, pressed back into the cushions, as though to distance themselves from Jules. Jules straightened back up, his eyes blazing with mad panic or anger.

"Don't," Richard warned, slowly standing himself. "Whatever it is you are considering right now, don't do it. It will only make things worse."

Jules took a breath, then stood more erect. "I do not know what you mean, Monsieur. Mademoiselle Banks is quite wrong."

"No," Penelope said, shaking her head slowly. "No, I am not."

"What is going on?" Simon asked, stalking over.

That triggered something for Jules, and he tried running. André, much younger and more lithe than his partner, easily caught him. For once, his quick and temperamental reaction was useful.

That was the moment that everyone in the car realized Jules was the murderer. Gasps and short screams erupted. Most people shot up from their seats. All eyes were on the young man struggling in André's grip. Jules no longer maintained a pretense of innocence. Right then, he was mad with anger at having been discovered.

"You are caught, Jules," Simon said, walking over to help his partner hold the man. "The only thing left to do is confess. Tell us where the Golden Monkey is."

Jules coughed out a sharp laugh, it unraveled into demented laughter. Penelope could see the frustration on the faces of Simon and André, realizing they would never get an answer from him.

"At least tell us how you knew, Mademoiselle Banks," Simon asked through gritted teeth. "Perhaps we can discover the whereabouts that way."

Penelope thought it rather tactless to focus so heavily on the Golden Monkey of Kashmir when there was still a dead body on the train. Of course, that dead body was no longer a mystery to solve, so she understood.

"Really, it's a matter of timing. I'm surprised I didn't think of one of the concierges to begin with. Of course, with so many of my fellow passengers leaving during dinner, and so many of them quite obviously either hiding something," she turned to Margaret and Edward, "or with a connection to Monsieur Barbier," she turned to Francine and Lucien, "it was understandable that the focus would remain on them."

Penelope paced, piecing together the timeline in her head. "It would have been when he was smoking in between the first and second cars that the opportunity first struck. There is a window into the next car one can see through when one is in the passageway. He must have seen Quentin leave to get Monsieur Barbier's dinner. That meant there was no concierge to witness anything. I'm not sure how much the concierges were told about Aristide beforehand." Pen turned to briefly consider Jules, who gave nothing away in his expression.

"We only told them that he was a person of interest transporting a valuable artifact that we hoped to recover."

"Which is certainly enough," Lulu said.

Pen nodded in agreement, then continued. "All the concierge's have master keys to each compartment. You entered Aristide's room, perhaps assuming he was still at dinner. Either that, or he was gone to place the real Golden Monkey in his other compartment and returned to find you inside. Whichever scenario is correct, you were caught and you realized your only solution was to kill him. Of course there was a struggle. That's when Edward and Margaret must have tried breaking in. When they heard his voice saying how dare you, I believe he was talking to you. It was when they left that you finally killed him. You took advantage of a weapon that was handy, the letter opener." Penelope turned to Quentin. "You say you saw Aristide retrieve the tray that you left for him. Did you actually see him or just his hand reach out to pull it into the room?"

"Only his hand," Quentin said, his eyes still wide at the prospect that one of his colleagues was possibly a murderer.

"I don't believe that was Aristide's hand, but that of Jules. Monsieur Barbier had removed his jacket at dinner, leaving him in a white dress shirt. It would have been very similar to the shirts the concierges have under their own uniformed jackets. All Jules would have had to do was remove his jacket and reach a hand out to pull in the tray."

"Of course," Honorine said, studying Jules.

Penelope sighed and threw her hands up in defeat. "From there, it becomes murky. I assume he stole one of the Golden Monkeys, but I can't say how he got the second.

Frankly, it could be an entirely different suspect you are looking for in the theft."

Jules grinned, a low chuckle emanating from his throat. "You will never find the real Golden Monkey." André gripped him harder either by impulse or anger. Jules hissed in pain, but it only made him laugh again.

"Are you looking to make a deal for a lighter sentence? Is that it?" Simon asked, a note of empathy in his voice. Penelope assumed it was to make Jules think he was sympathetic to his plight.

"His fingerprints will be somewhere in that room, probably still on the murder weapon," Penelope said.

Jules just shot her a look so smug, she knew he had been smart enough to at least wipe away any prints from the letter opener. "You'll never find it. Consider it gone. You can tear this train apart, piece by piece—and that's if the company allows it, which they won't—I'll still be the only one who knows where it is."

André cursed in French and twisted Jules's arm, such that he hissed in pain once again.

"Non, André," Simon said, though without an ounce of sympathy in his voice this time. *"There are more effective means."* He leaned in to look Jules in the eye. "You will spend many years in prison, perhaps so long that the Golden Monkey will either be found or will be of no value to you."

A gleam came to Jules's eye. "That is where you are wrong."

CHAPTER THIRTY-FIVE

Penelope interpreted Jules's response just before Simon did. If Jules did go to prison for murder, even on a lesser charge of manslaughter, he would be away for quite some time. If the Golden Monkey was still on the train, that would certainly be long enough to discover its whereabouts. So why was Jules so self satisfied about them either never finding it, or it having some value to him before he was ever released from prison?

"I am wrong? Ah, I see." Simon gave André a cheerful look. "Our concierge hopes to make a deal. Perhaps no prison at all? For such an important international artifact, surely such a request would be accommodated?"

Penelope felt her outrage set in before she realized Simon was teasing Jules.

"You want it, badly enough to make the deal. Your International Criminal Police Commission is still new. Failing at such an important case would not look good."

"Nor would allowing a murderer to go free," Simon said curtly.

Jules gave him an incredulous look. "We both know you are willing to bend the rules when it comes to getting what you want." He cast a quick glance toward Lucien.

Rather than get angry, Simon relaxed and his demeanor became pleasant once again. "Hiring a...consultant is hardly the same as being lenient with a murderer."

"If I did it, I would be smart enough to realize that I would not go unpunished. I would also be smart enough to know I could earn myself a favorable sentence." He gave Simon a piercing look.

Simon studied him for a moment. "If you did it, how exactly would it have been done?"

Jules laughed. "Do you think I am stupid?"

"If I may...?" Honorine said, drawing everyone's attention. She sauntered over, giving Jules an assessing look. "The very astute Mademoiselle Banks has already revealed the major aspects of your crime. You knew of the Golden Monkey, or at least knew of some valuable artifact beforehand. Then, you simply took advantage of a window of opportunity. The murder is easy enough to explain, as I do not think you intended it. Monsieur Barbier simply caught you in the act, and you silenced him with a weapon that was conveniently available to you at the time, the letter opener."

Any bit of appreciation Penelope felt at Honorine's compliment was quickly eroding. After all, Honorine was simply restating everything she had already revealed.

As though reading her mind, Honorine turned to give Pen a knowing smile. "The only mystery left to solve is with regard to the location of the Golden Monkey." She turned back to Jules with a speculative look, then began pacing. "You are an opportunist. I do not think you would have the eye to tell a real from a fake. No, no, you simply take what is presented. Thus, it must have come as quite the surprise to return to Monsieur Barbier's room and discover yet another Golden Monkey. After all, you had already taken one after murdering him, non? One that was in the room with him at the time....or no." She shook her head and gave him an overtly sympathetic look. "You discovered there was no Golden Monkey when you first entered. That must have been quite frustrating, especially after committing the unforgivable sin." Her eyes brightened. "But then you remembered Monsieur Barbier had a second compartment, for which you conveniently had the key. It was also quite convenient that the third car was temporarily without a concierge—" She turned to give Adrien a reassuring look. "One who was, ah, perhaps attending to his housekeeping duties? All the better for you to quickly open the door to that second compartment...et voilà! There was the Golden Monkey!" Her brow rose and her glittering dark eyes widened. "But alas! Later on, you must have remembered one small thing, the very thing that might have the guillotine removing your head from your body." She made a sound and ran her hand horizontally across her neck.

"Oh my," Cousin Cordelia said.

Honorine turned to give her a wink. "Not to worry, ma cherie." She spun back to face Jules. "Our concierge made sure to erase the evidence of his presence in Monsieur Barbier's room. *That* is why you returned, to wipe your fingerprints from the scene and the letter opener. Et voilà! To your surprise, another Golden Monkey has appeared! But which was real and which was fake? This time, you were more ingenious. You could not count on passing through several cars unnoticed, as most passengers had returned from dinner. So, you once again used what was conveniently available to you, Monsieur Barbier's suitcase.

A simple note, a few francs, and it would be safely off the train, awaiting your retrieval when the voyage was over."

Jules stared at Honorine, his face unreadable. As someone who catered to a demanding clientele, he had perfected his ability to respond to surprise or unpleasantness with a neutral reaction. Really, the how and why did not matter. He had been the only one with means and opportunity to carry out every step of the murder and theft.

Honorine turned to Penelope. "You see, mademoiselle, you were correct all along. Eventually you would have come to the same conclusion."

Penelope felt her face warm. She had all but stated as much, but failed to tie it to the second Golden Monkey. Now, it all made sense.

"That is all very interesting," Simon said dryly. "And yet, we do not have the second Golden Monkey."

"And you never will," Jules stated in a matter-of-fact manner.

Pen's mind instantly went to work. She had been so close to piecing it all together before Honorine swooped in to do it. She felt a competitive bug buzzing around in her head, encouraging her to find the whereabouts of the Golden Monkey, quite possibly the real one.

She immediately dismissed the most obvious locations. A search of every compartment was certain to take place, even the empty ones—especially the empty ones. No, it would be some place more discreet.

Or perhaps it would be hiding in plain sight?

Or perhaps in a location so obscure, Jules was right about no one finding it.

Pineapples! For all Penelope knew it was on the roof of the very carriage they were in at the moment, being held there with glue.

Penelope felt the pressure of the moment put an ache in her head. The silence of the car told her that everyone was waiting for her to magically find an answer. It wasn't even her place to solve the case. Perhaps she should for once have taken Richard's advice to leave it to the proper authorities.

However....

There were still a few hours before they reached Lyon. Jules's smug look of satisfaction was enough to spur her. She wanted nothing more than to do the very thing that would wipe that look from his face. He was sure to use the mysterious location as a bargaining chip.

Penelope closed her eyes and replayed the evening in her head. Specifically all the areas Jules would have had access to. She hadn't seen him in the present car, at least not until the murder was discovered and everyone gathered. Besides, he wouldn't have been comfortable hiding it so far away, and in a place so frequented by passengers.

That left the first car he served, the second he had direct access to, and possibly the third car, which would have been far, but mostly unpopulated. Beyond the first car were staffing areas, including the car that housed the conductors and engineers. Far too risky.

Now that she had narrowed down the location, she scrolled through every photographic image in her head. What seemed odd or different? It was impossible to say. This was her first time traveling the line, so she couldn't say with any certainty what was out of place or unusual. If Jules hadn't told her he was not allowed to smoke, she wouldn't have even considered that strange. She thought back to that odor she'd had to wade through, the odor that had cinched the case. Cigarette smoke had never made her eyes water, especially well after the smoker had left. What had made that happen?

This, of course, made her think of Lucien's lighter. It was obvious Jules had stolen it, but why? She thought of the match Jules had used to light Lucien's cigarette. It burned quicker than a lighter, often forcing users to strike another match if they needed a longer flame life. And Lucien's lighter fluid had been mostly used up.

So what had Jules used it for? What was the connection between a Golden Monkey and a long-lasting flame? Zounds, that only made her head ache even more. Pen would have been hard pressed to find two more distinctly different things, let alone how they were connected.

Penelope's eyes suddenly shot to the dining room, where Pierre sat. She thought of his book. He was no doubt hoping to remain unnoticed, perhaps long enough to liberate the bonds from between the pages of his book—the pages pasted together with a glue strong enough to make eyes water.

When Penelope stalked over to the dining room and flung open the doors, Monsieur Padou was so startled, he nearly fell out of his chair. He was even more shocked when Penelope closed the distance and leaned in to sniff the book.

"What are you doing?" Pierre demanded, placing a protective hand on it.

"I would like to know as well," Simon said, having followed her there, leaving Jules in the hands of André. He snatched the book away from Pierre, giving him a wary glance before opening it and flipping through the pages.

"I think we're all curious," Richard said, giving Pen a puzzled look.

"Glue!" Pen said with satisfaction. "It was mostly hidden underneath the smell of cigarette smoke, but the physical effects of it lingered, namely making my eyes water." She pointed at the book. "I knew something about this smell was familiar."

She returned to the lounge to address Quentin, who still stared at Jules as though he was Benedict Arnold himself. "There is glue on board the train somewhere, no?"

"Er, yes," he said finally tearing his eyes away from Jules. "In the car between yours and the engine room, the train holds any matter of supplies and tools, including glue."

"What does that have to do with the whereabouts of the Golden Monkey?" Simon asked, not bothering to hide his skepticism.

Once again, Penelope felt her confusion and doubt set in. She would have assumed she was on the wrong path, save for a quick glance toward Jules, who was still being held by André. The secure look of satisfaction had faded. He was worried.

Pen figured she might as well ask the others. She looked around the lounge. "What would someone need a lighter and glue for?"

At first, she was only met with blank faces, but then she saw a few people begin to consider the question.

"Most glue is pretty flammable. One could start a pretty serious fire with it," Richard offered, a doubtful wrinkle in his brow. Some had a look of alarm at the idea but, as there had yet been no fire, they dismissed that danger.

"Hobbies," Edward posed. "Many hobbies like woodworking or model making require glue and some sort of heat."

Pen nodded in consideration. Jules could have crafted something to hide the Golden Monkey in, but that seemed like a lot of effort. The glue was understandable if he was ripping something open and wanted to put it back together to hide the object. But why did he need the lighter? Could it have possibly been completely unrelated to the Golden Monkey? Perhaps the man was simply a pathological thief? The lighter did look valuable. However, that didn't explain why so much lighter fluid had been used.

She glanced at Jules to read his face. The smug look was back, this time with a sneer added. He was enjoying himself. At her resulting frown, a low laugh began in his throat.

"Is this funny to you, Jules?"

His laughter became more pronounced before he answered. "It is indeed. Watching you hopelessly struggle almost makes it worthwhile. For once, something isn't handed to you in life. Everyday I cater to people like you who see right past me in their incessant demands of champagne and softer pillows. Even this silly Golden Monkey. It was probably made as some gift to another member of the ruling classes, something he didn't even need, while the common people below him no doubt starved. I would have liked the money—if I had stolen it." A taunting smile curled his lips. "As it is, I hope it is never found."

While the other passengers bristled at the insult, Penelope mentally pored over his words. One in particular had sparked something from the images in her head.

Once again, Penelope addressed the room. "Did anyone order champagne be brought to their room after the dinner service?"

Most eyes turned to Honorine, including Pen's. She pretended to look mildly offended before being the first to answer. "*Moi? Non.*"

"Anyone else?" Penelope scanned the room to find every head shaking.

Penelope felt her chest swell and her heart beat faster as she realized she was on the right track. One look at Jules was enough to confirm it. His expression was now dour and his face a bit paler.

"I saw you setting down an open bottle of champagne on ice in your concierge station. At the time, just after dinner, I simply assumed that you had procured some for a passenger in another carriage in Quentin's absence. After all, no one in the first car had yet returned from dinner." Pen turned to look at Margaret. "Earlier you mentioned something about champagne."

Margaret flinched, either at the memory of her embarrassing display or at being so frankly questioned. "I...I did."

"When you flung your arm in the direction of the group of concierges, was it directed at one in particular?"

Margaret's eyes widened at the realization. "Yes, it was Jules. I saw him carrying a bucket with a bottle when Edward and I returned to our quarters. I assumed it was for Madame DuBois."

"Penelope dear, I still don't understand what champagne and lighters and all of these other things have to do with the Golden Monkey?" Cousin Cordelia protested.

Penelope turned to Simon. "Is the statue small enough to fit inside of a champagne bottle?"

Rather than answer, Simon's eyes widened, and he immediately left to get the bottle from the first carriage.

"I suppose that is a, '*oui*,'" Honorine said, beaming a congratulatory smile Penelope's way. "Very good, mademoiselle."

"I have to say, Pen honey, I'm also a bit confused. How did he get a Golden Monkey into a champagne bottle?" Lulu asked.

Penelope grinned. "I read about it in a crafting book when I was a girl. How to reuse household items. For example, making hurricane glasses out of old bottles. First, you score them around the bottom—surely there is a tool on this train sharp enough to etch through glass."

"Yes, as I stated, we have tools for nearly every general use," Quentin confirmed.

"Naturally," Pen continued. "From there, you simply heat the area for an extended period, either with boiling water or...a lighter," she turned to glance at Lucien. "The final step is to use ice to cool it, and the bottom should come apart without shattering the glass. An open champagne bottle sitting on ice is hardly suspect. I imagine there were at least one or two empty bottles available for him to pilfer. After it was open, he simply placed the Golden Monkey inside and then glued it back together, stuffing it back into the ice bucket so no one was the wiser."

"I suppose in that regard, I am quite guilty of abetting," Honorine said pleasantly. She cast a teasing look Jules way. "Who knew my love of champagne would enable such a clever bit of disguise."

The concierge was sullen and quiet, all hints of boasting and sneering completely erased from his face. By now, he knew the jig was up and the only smart move left to him was to remain quiet.

"I hope your fiancée was worth it."

He gave Penelope a withering look that made her wonder if there even was a woman he planned to marry at all. It made for a sympathetic story, one he probably used to encourage more tips from passengers.

Simon rushed in, holding up the open champagne bottle triumphantly. When he smashed it against the side of the bar, Penelope and everyone else winced at the sound of it breaking apart. However, they all then rushed in to get a better look as a small item, wrapped in a bit of cloth (no doubt to buffer the noise of the statue clanking against the glass) fell to the floor. Simon was quick to pick it up and unwrap it. He held up the item inside for everyone's inspection, a broad smile on his face.

The Golden Monkey of Kashmir grinned back at them, its emerald eyes twinkling with mischief, as though it was fully aware of the chaos it had created and found the whole thing highly amusing.

EPILOGUE

The police presence that greeted them at the Lyon station a little after six in the morning was substantial. There was no doubt an equally large media presence being held back further in the station. Penelope wondered if it was too late in the morning for all the facts to make it to press for that day's papers.

At the very least, a few evening editions of the French and international papers would have an eye-catching headline to present to the world. A concierge for one of France's most prominent rail lines was a thief and a murderer. That, combined with a valuable artifact that lay at the center of the case made it something any reporter would salivate over. If the looks on the faces of the other non-First Class passengers, who had just received the news, was any indication, the public would be even more eager to devour the story.

"Your liaisons are mighty pleased with themselves," Penelope said, watching André and Simon coordinate handing over Jules and Pierre Padou to the local police in Lyon.

"I don't think they will be my liaisons much longer,"

Richard said. "I don't particularly approve of their methods of policing."

She didn't disagree with him. It was one thing for a private investigator to operate without reins, but there was a reason regulations and procedures existed for police officers. They had far more power and authority with which to operate, and it behooved them to avoid consorting with such unsavory characters like Lucien.

"I think perhaps you should coordinate with them for the moment. Who knows what they are telling the police right now? At the very least, try to keep me from becoming too involved, darling. I'm happy to let them take *most* of the credit, if only to avoid any messy entanglements with the International Criminal Police Commission."

Richard smiled, then kissed her cheek before wandering to where the police were still encircled around Jules in handcuffs.

Penelope took a moment to observe the other passengers before wandering back to her friends.

Edward and Margaret were talking with Francine. Penelope was certain she was giving them as much information as possible to help recover their mother's money. If she had Aristide's bank account information, anything else she knew would be quite valuable in that endeavor. At the very least, they had a very capable French private investigator who would no doubt make sure justice prevailed.

Penelope gave a sympathetic smile to Jules and Adrien, who were consoling one another. One of her caveats to André and Simon was that she wanted the reward money for finding the Golden Monkey of Kashmir. She fully planned on dividing it between Adrien, who may have looked forward to an early retirement, and Quentin, who could use the money to help his sickly father.

Lucien seemed perfectly placid as he smoked a cigarette in solitude. His profession was one of wins or losses, and he didn't seem bothered by this particular loss. There would always be other stolen objects in the world for him to find and reap the rewards.

Honorine was with Benny, Lulu, and Cousin Cordelia. They all laughed at something she had just said to them, though Penelope's cousin blushed furiously as she did.

"What joke have I missed?" Penelope asked as she joined them.

"I was simply telling them of my adventures uncovering a murder that took place underneath a *Moulin* of a certain color. The heights to which I had to kick my foot in the air just to operate undercover at that particular establishment..." She waggled her eyebrows and grinned, as though she had enjoyed herself more than she really should have on that case.

It fascinated Penelope to no end. Her own adventures in private investigating had led her into certain risqué situations, but the Belle Epoque period in Paris during which Honorine had first worked must have been quite thrilling.

"I see our police peacocks have their feathers quite fanned," Honorine said, looking past Penelope to where the police were all congratulating themselves.

"I'm just happy that the murderer was caught."

"Indeed."

"The champagne is on me when we reach Paris," Benny said, then sported a devilish smile. "Speaking of provocative shows, I can't wait to see this Josephine Baker live. I do so love the more liberated European sensibilities."

"I'll just be happy to meet her," Lulu said.

"I simply want to see Paris again," Cousin Cordelia said, a smile of sentimental fondness coming to her face.

"Paris is quite magical," Honorine agreed. She turned to Pen with sudden interest. "I wonder if perhaps I might speak to you in private?"

"Of course," Pen said, curiosity striking her. The other three seemed just as curious, but they urged the two of them to step away.

"What is it?"

Honorine pursed her lips as though wondering what to say. She tilted her head to consider Penelope. "I wanted you to know that your secret is quite safe with me."

"My secret?" Pen's brow wrinkled in puzzlement.

"You are not yet married, *non*?"

"That's hardly a secret," Penelope said with a laugh.

"Ahh…" Honorine nodded with understanding. "Yes, we are most certainly in a progressive era, however…."

"However, what?" Pen said, suddenly serious again.

"You do recall me stating that I have quite a few nieces and nephews?"

"Yes…?" Penelope said, a sudden dread overcoming her.

"Well…"

"No!"

"*Oui*," Honorine said, a sympathetic smile coming to her face. "You have the same glow your beautiful mother did when I met her. Alors…*félicitations*?"

Penelope felt suddenly lightheaded. So many little things about this European tour suddenly made sense. She had attributed it all to a change in environment and the stress of travel, not to mention several murder cases.

As it turned out, she was going to be…a mother!

AUTHOR NOTES

HONORINE

To answer the question before it is asked, *yes* (!) I am thinking of a murder mystery series for Honorine DuBois. I have just as much a love affair with the Belle Epoque period as I do the 1920s. However, the research is far more elaborate—mostly due to my lack of French fluency. Still, the bug has bitten me. As this story suggests, I have already started working on her first murder mystery, though I hope to add many more. Oh, what a fun adventure it will be!

THE BLUE TRAIN

What is a historical murder mystery series without one of the mysteries taking place on a train? The blue train in this book is based on the famous train of the same color that was one of the luxurious sleeper trains by the Compagnie Internationale des Wagons-Lits (the same company that runs the more famous Orient Express). Agatha Christie herself penned a murder—far less famous than that novel set on the Orient Express—that took place on this very

AUTHOR NOTES

train. It ran from the 1880s to the 1970s and the conductors (called concierges in this book) all had to speak at least three languages, and all notices were written in French, German, Italian, and English.

Continue to Get Your Free Book...

GET YOUR FREE BOOK!

Mischief at The Peacock Club

A bold theft at the infamous Peacock Club. Can Penelope solve it to save her own neck?

1924 New York
Penelope "Pen" Banks has spent the past two years making ends meet by playing cards. It's another Saturday night at The Peacock Club, one of her favorite haunts, and she has

GET YOUR FREE BOOK!

her sights set on a big fish, who just happens to be the special guest of the infamous Jack Sweeney.

After inducing Rupert Cartland, into a game of cards, Pen thinks it just might be her lucky night. Unfortunately, before the night ends, Rupert has been robbed—his diamond cuff links, ruby pinky ring, gold watch, and wallet...all gone!

With The Peacock Club's reputation on the line, Mr. Sweeney, aided by the heavy hand of his chief underling Tommy Callahan, is holding everyone captive until the culprit is found.

For the promise of a nice payoff, not to mention escaping the club in one piece, Penelope Banks is willing to put her unique mind to work to find out just who stole the goods.

This is a prequel novella to the *Penelope Banks Murder Mysteries* series, taking place at The Peacock Club before Penelope Banks became a private investigator.

Access your book at the link below:
https://dl.bookfunnel.com/4sv9fir4h3

ALSO BY COLETTE CLARK

PENELOPE BANKS MURDER MYSTERIES

A Murder in Long Island

The Missing White Lady

Pearls, Poison & Park Avenue

Murder in the Gardens

A Murder in Washington Square

The Great Gaston Murder

A Murder After Death

A Murder on 34th Street

Spotting A Case of Murder

The Girls and the Golden Egg

Murder on the Atlantic

A Murder on the Côte D'Azure

A Murder in Blue

LISETTE DARLING GOLDEN AGE MYSTERIES

A Sparkling Case of Murder

A Murder on Sunset Boulevard

A Murder Without Motive

The Cat and the Cadaver

ABOUT THE AUTHOR

Colette Clark lives in New York and has always enjoyed learning more about the history of her amazing city. She decided to combine that curiosity and love of learning with her addiction to reading and watching mysteries. Her first series, **Penelope Banks Murder Mysteries** is the result of those passions. When she's not writing she can be found doing Sudoku puzzles, drawing, eating tacos, visiting museums dedicated to unusual/weird/wacky things, and, of course, reading mysteries by other great authors.

Join my Newsletter to receive news about New Releases and Sales!
https://dashboard.mailerlite.com/forms/148684/72678356487767318/share

Printed in Great Britain
by Amazon